STORNOWAY PRIMARY
WESTERN ISLES LIBRARIES

ANNA LEWINS

CROW'S HEAD

PUFFIN BOOKS
in association with Blackie and Son Ltd

PUFFIN BOOKS

Published by the Penguin Group
Penguin Books Ltd, 27 Wrights Lane, London W8 5TZ, England
Penguin Books USA Inc., 375 Hudson Street, New York, New York 10014, USA
Penguin Books Australia Ltd, Ringwood, Victoria, Australia
Penguin Books Canada Ltd, 10 Alcorn Avenue, Toronto, Ontario, Canada M4V 3B2
Penguin Books (NZ) Ltd, 182–190 Wairau Road, Auckland 10, New Zealand

Penguin Books Ltd, Registered Offices: Harmondsworth, Middlesex, England

First published by Blackie and Son Ltd 1990
Published in Puffin Books 1992
1 3 5 7 9 10 8 6 4 2

Printed in England by Clays Ltd, St Ives plc

Contents

1 Bird Island   7

2 The Gang   21

3 Crow's Head   33

4 Something Nasty   46

5 Dark Waters   57

6 Ceilidh   70

7 Silver Beak   81

8 Josh in Trouble   96

9 In the Well   107

10 Night of the Poison Cat   120

11 The Birds   132

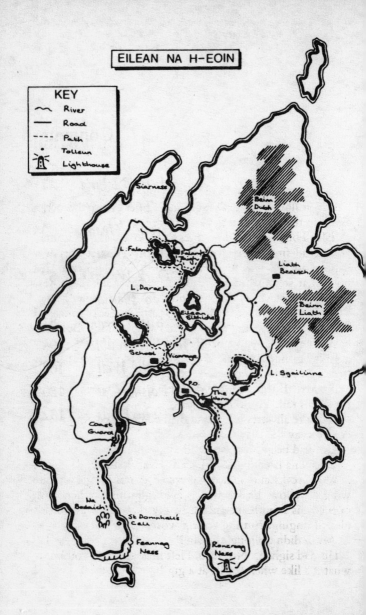

EILEAN NA H-EOIN

KEY
~~~ River
—— Road
--- Path
Telleun
Lighthouse

Siarness

Beinn Dubh

L. Falanie

L. Darach

Liath Bealach

Eilean Slábhichd

Beinn Liath

School   Vionnag

L. Sgailinne

P.O.

The

Coast Guard

Na Bodaich

St Domhnall's Cell

Feannag Ness

Ronenag Ness

1 Bird Island

'They're coming! Look, they're flying to meet us!'

Josh followed Ishbel's pointing finger, over the ocean and into the afternoon sky. 'What are they?'

'Island birds. They'd no miss a chance to sing us home.'

For the first time, Josh really believed that this was happening. He was really going to live on an island that no one at school had heard of. Ishbel was his dad's new wife, the new Mrs Williams, and the island was her home.

'If they haven't got TV . . .' Josh frowned. 'I mean, I don't mind being the only black kid in school. But they have seen black people before?'

Ishbel grinned at him. 'Ach, we do read the newspapers, Josh. They'll no think you're from Mars.'

'Funny.' But Josh felt better. He braced his ribs against the ship's rail. 'Are they seagulls?'

'They're all sorts of gulls and all come to see you. Now, can you say the island's name, yet?'

Josh had been practising. 'Ill . . . Onion?'

'Eilean na h-eoin – Bird Island. Hear them sing!'

Wild creaks and squeals swooped down on grey-white wings, yellow beaks wide, eyes glinting. When Josh opened his mouth, he meant to say that this was not his idea of singing. But the wrong words came out.

'Mum didn't phone, did she?'

His dad sighed. 'No, Josh. I left messages but you know what it's like when Carl's at a gig.'

Josh nodded. A week ago, he had stood in the registry office and watched his dad marry Ishbel. His dad had let him loose in his favourite clothes shop to buy new trainers, brilliant socks, a really smart jacket and a round black-leather hat. The hat was magic. So how come he felt so awful now? He suddenly felt sick – seasick and homesick.

'Are you all right, Josh?' Ishbel had asked him that ten times since they'd left London.

He backed away from her. 'I just need to walk about a bit.'

His dad called after him. 'You be careful, Josh. Don't fall overboard.'

When Ishbel and Josh's dad stood close together, they looked more white and more black. Ishbel was not even pretty, just a slim, brown-haired white woman with hazel eyes. Josh wondered what his dad saw in her. His dad was handsome, even the kids at school said so. He had a smart moustache and wore clothes Josh would like to pinch for himself. But Josh's mum had still gone off with Carl Benjamin. Josh had not seen her since the divorce, three years ago. He had to read about her in the papers.

Chin crunched into his chest, Josh slouched around the ferry. The boat had chugged along for eight hours. In summer, it steamed to the island every fortnight with mail and supplies. In winter, it came once a month and then sometimes gave up because of storms. And no TV! No pop videos! He would go crazy! Josh glared at the seagulls dive-bombing his shoulders.

'Just try it, fish-breath!' He ducked as another gull swept past. 'Go on, try it!'

The next bird did. It flew right at him and shrieked into his ear. Josh yelped and blundered backwards, colliding into the woman with the cat-basket. He nearly lost his specs. Her elbow flattened his nose. He was a big boy, tall as well as fat, and no other twelve year old in his school had been able to knock him over. The woman bounced off him and sat on the deck.

'Shoot! I'm sorry . . .' He held his hand out.

The woman's eyes stared at his hand, then crawled up his new padded jacket to his black-hatted face. Her mouth gaped open. The rest of her face was nothing special, small and grey, but someone had threaded invisible elastic through the left corner of her mouth and tied it, tight, to her left eyebrow. Her mouth was twisted upwards, the brow twisted downwards. Her clothes were horrible.

'You!' She surged to her feet. Bits of spit fizzed on her lips. 'You're too late!' And she lunged at him.

'Hoi!' Josh dodged sideways. 'Hey!'

Her fingers clutched his sleeve and he ducked the other way. No time to think. When she came at him again, Josh staggered into the rail. His feet skidded away from him, his arms waved, he tried to yell. Her crooked mouth swam closer, tongue flicking yellow teeth. Her hands clawed for his throat. And a bird slammed into her face. Black. Big and black. A crow, Josh thought. Something wrong with its beak. Its raucous screech nearly deafened him. A gull cracked off her shoulder, another off her chest, and she stumbled, covering her face with her hands. Josh scrabbled upright and slithered into a mad, head-down sprint.

'Josh!' Ishbel had waited for him. 'Are you all right?'

That made it eleven times.

'Where's Dad?' Josh could not believe what had just happened. 'Where is he?'

'Inside. You look like a wee, lost puppy!' She frowned into his eyes. 'You're no scared about school, surely?'

Funny. Someone had just tried to kill him and Ishbel

thought he was scared about school. He still could not believe it. He heard himself gabble a load of rubbish.

'Nah, that's OK. It'll be great wearing my own things instead of a uniform.' His back hurt where he had crashed into the rail. 'I'm getting a gang together. Then I'll have friends straight away. It'll be the best gang ever.' He clutched the rail until his knees stopped quivering. 'It'll be great.'

An hour later, the ferry bobbed into Roncamas Caladh, the island's wide lagoon of a harbour. Feannag Ness towered to the left with its circle of prehistoric stones – great, grey slabs jutting into the sky. The islanders called them Na Bodaich – the Old Men.

'Na Bodaich . . . It's like Stonehenge.' Josh was impressed. 'Did I say the Gaelic right?'

'As right as any islander says it, Josh. Island Gaelic is different. We have our own way of speaking, our own way of everything.' Ishbel smiled. 'Folk here are very special.'

The ferry slowed, tipping from wave to wave, and Josh glanced to his right. Rocks studded the eastern shore of the harbour and plump, grey-brown bodies lazed there, a whole herd of sleek blubber.

'Dad, look! Dad, they're seals!'

'That's why the town's called Roncamas – Seal Bay.' Ishbel pointed over the seal-dotted rocks. 'And there's the Worm.'

His new home. It looked cold – a two-storey pub, white-washed and black-roofed, a pebble beach below it with a stiff, wooden thumb of pier pointing into the water.

The ferry nudged into the main quay. Immediately,

10

two women jumped onto the deck – one pretty, red-haired woman in a flowery dress and shawl, one ginger woman whose jacket had more badges than a scout master's. They waited, grinning at Ishbel and Josh and Nathan Williams, not knowing what to say.

'Now here's Fiona and Janet come to meet us!' Ishbel pushed Josh forwards. 'This is Joshua . . . And Nathan . . . And I'm that glad to see you, I could burst!'

Josh forgot the women's names as soon as he heard them. He wanted to check if Roncamas was as small as it looked. Most of the buildings stood one storey high, either white-walled with black roofs or black-walled with grassy, shaggy roofs as if the thatch had sprouted. It was like one of those documentary films: *Primitive Life in the Grot Islands*.

The buildings stretched around half of the bay from the lifeboat house on the left, to the pub out on its own on the right. Josh had started to ask who had chosen the pub's stupid name – The Worm Turns – when his neck prickled ice-cold. He stepped back too fast, onto his dad's feet.

'Ow! Josh! You're too heavy for that!'

And Ishbel's voice turned sharp as glass. 'What are you doing here, Morag Falamh? You know you're no welcome here.'

The woman with the cat-basket smirked, crookedly.

'You've never!' Ishbel's ginger friend pointed at the cat-basket. 'You never have!'

'Why don't you look, Janet Doinnean?' Morag threw the basket at the other woman's feet. 'There's no law says I canna bring a cat home.' Spit glistened on her chin.

'There's the island law!' Ishbel pulled Josh against her, her arm around his middle. 'No cats . . . You wouldn't dare!'

11

'She'd dare anything, she's that twisted.' Janet dropped onto her knees and tore the basket open. 'You auld, crabbit . . . !' She glared at Morag Falamh. 'You evil witch!'

Josh goggled at the basket and the white, arched chain of bone and rib inside. Not a cat, a cat's skeleton.

A car horn blasted and the crowd on the pier muttered and scowled, shuffling aside.

'They're never still here?' Ishbel watched the car stop and its two passengers smile out at her. 'I thought they'd have gone, by now.'

Josh took a good, hard stare – posh car, flash suits. Whoever the men were, he did not like them.

'They're guests of mine.' Morag lifted the basket and snapped the lid shut. 'As long as I own this place, I'll have any guest I choose. And you'll be right sorry you called me a witch, Janet Doinnean. You'll all be sorry for how you've treated the Falamhs!'

From all sides, cold eyes, dark glares surrounded her, but Morag enjoyed it. She folded onto the back seat and the big car sped away.

Ishbel frowned. 'She's up to something, that sleekit auld besom! What did she bring that horrendous monstrosity here for?'

'Those men have been over every stone and tussock on the island.' Janet shuddered. 'It's no natural.'

Josh's dad had controlled himself for five minutes. Now his eyebrows shot up and he pulled one of his funny faces. 'What's all this about cats? And her owning the island?'

'We have no cats here, Nathan, nothing that kills birds.' Ishbel sighed. 'And the Falamhs do own the island. They cheated us out of it, years ago.'

The gentle breeze changed direction without warning, flying in cold from the sea.

'Rain's coming. We'd best get to the Worm.' Ishbel found her smile again. 'Now, we'll see you both this evening, won't we?'

'We'll come to wish you luck.' The red-haired woman – Fiona – kissed Josh on the chin, making him jump and wriggle. 'Welcome to Eilean na h-eoin, Josh and Nathan.'

'And here's Willy-John to drive you home.' Ginger Janet pointed to the old man at the end of the pier. 'Let's help with those cases.'

Josh lugged his own cases along the pier, nodding to people until his neck ached. Behind him, his dad pushed Josh's bike with one hand, carried the heaviest case with the other. Josh had reached the pier-end when he saw that Willy-John had not brought a car to meet them. The old man perched on the high seat of a pony-drawn cart.

'Hey!' Josh pointed at the two, hairy ponies. 'Are they ours?'

Ishbel smiled. 'Remember, Josh, there aren't many cars on the island. We've ponies and traps for the summer, land-rovers for the winter, bicycles for whenever the storms don't blow. Hurry, now, we're keeping your granny waiting.'

Josh had almost forgotten. Ishbel's mum lived at the hotel as well.

Willy-John grunted. 'So, you're the son of the house? An auld Bible name, is it?'

'Joshua,' Josh said. 'But everyone calls me Josh. Any chance of a ride up there?'

The old man's face crinkled. 'Aye, come on up. So long as you dinna blether while I'm driving.'

'I won't . . . blether.' Josh hauled himself onto the wooden seat. 'Hey, this is magic! Can I learn to drive the ponies, Ishbel?'

'You can do anything you like, m'eudail. Willy-John, you be looking after my boy, there.'

Willy-John clicked his tongue and the ponies walked forwards. 'Now, this laddie can fend for himself, I'm thinking. He's a good set of bones on him.'

That was the nicest thing anyone had said about Josh's heavy body. Ishbel had called him 'm'eudail' – 'my darling'. She was not his real mum and he had only known her for a few months. But he liked the way she had stood up to that Morag woman.

The first drop of rain blobbed Josh's nose. He rubbed it dry as Willy-John steered on to the bay road. A row of shops separated road from water. Nearly falling off his seat, Josh peered into the windows . . . Woolly jumpers! Woolly hats! Woolly everything! A large, black bird huddled on a shop roof, watching him. Josh blinked and the bird had gone, but he knew he had seen it.

Willy-John nodded forwards. 'This is the main road through Roncamas. The Worm's just the other side of Sgailinburn.'

What Josh needed was a map of the island. He knew that a burn was a stream, Ishbel had told him that. Feet bobbing above the ponies' tails, he let his mind wander. The white pub walls looked whiter with dark clouds behind them. A bit like Ishbel looking whiter when his dad put an arm around her. Then Josh saw the burn cutting down a rocky waterfall, and a pile of stones.

'What's that?' Josh pointed to the stones. 'And that . . . There's two of them.'

Rain spattered the grey rocks.

'Ach, that's the good luck of the Worm,' Willy-John said. 'We've two tolleun to tend. There's always tolleun at meeting places. It could be where road meets road, or burn meets burn. It's where two worlds join, you see. A powerful place.'

'Yeah, but what's a tolleun?'

Willy-John stared at him. 'You dinna know? A tolleun's a holy place for the island birds. If a bird feels itself dying, that's where it rests its poor, wee wings.'

'Great.' Josh swallowed. 'I'm glad I asked.'

He scowled at the stony heaps. Sure enough, feathers and bird-droppings dotted the round stones. But so did dried flowers, pieces of ribbon and lace, paper threaded on string.

'Dad. . . ?' Some weirdo had been decorating the stones. 'Dad . . . ?'

A bird-cry cut through his voice and something smacked the back of his head. He expected to see the crow. Instead, a gull the size of a spaniel clung to Ishbel's shoulder, its webbed feet tangling her scarf, its yellow beak digging into her hair.

'Ach, now stop that, Goath! Wheesht, man! Nathan, Josh, this is our house bird, Goath. He's come to welcome me back. And to look at the two of you.'

Josh forgot what he had been going to say. He gawped at her. 'Are you serious?'

The bird nibbled Ishbel's chin.

'You cannot be serious!'

'Josh, I told you the island was special.' Ishbel sighed. 'Goath, off with you. Go on, now. Up!'

Goath dragged himself into the air and onto the pub sign – a swinging board painted with a worm chasing a crow. He settled on one corner, folding his wings and squawking.

The cart clattered into the pub yard and Ishbel scrambled onto the wet cobbles.

'Watch this. Mam will be out before I reach—'

A woman exploded from behind the pub. Josh took her in at a glance – short grey hair, steel-rimmed specs, baggy trousers, a jumper down to her knees. She did not bother to slow down, simply pounced and threw Ishbel into the air.

'Ach, my bonny bairn! Have you missed your auld mam?' She did not wait for an answer. 'And this is Nathan! She said you were right handsome! I like a man with a moustache!'

To Josh's delight, Ishbel's mum lifted Nathan Williams into the air as well. Then Josh's grin faded.

'And the babbie of the family! My, he's a fine, big lad! Come and give your granny a kiss!'

Josh cringed. He hated to be slobbered over. With Willy-John chuckling behind him, he clambered into his gran's arms. She tossed him like a pancake and he came down giggling.

Ailsa dropped Josh back onto the cobbles. 'Now, come inside, this minute, and let's get something warm in your bellies. Come in out of the rain.'

Downstairs were the Worm's two bars, the larger one for smokers, the smaller, quiet one for people who wanted clean air around them. A door from the quiet bar led into a games room with billiards, table-tennis and skittles. Even better, the pub had its own, small swimming-pool in the cellar. Along the front hall, a door opened into the biggest room of all. A stage at one end supported an old piano and a few spotlights. Granny Ailsa said it was for wedding receptions and ceilidhs. Josh would see his first ceilidh on Saturday.

To Josh's delight, his room overlooked the seal colony. Common seals dropped their pups from June to July and he spent half an hour hanging over his window-sill, grinning at the fat, furry things. They barked like dogs and lay on their sides, scratching themselves with their flipper-tips. Magic.

That evening, islanders came from miles around to introduce themselves and ask questions. They wanted to know everything about Josh and his dad. He had never talked so much about himself in his life and his head spun. His dad started to look a bit odd, as well.

'Dustbin lids,' Nathan said to the little old lady with the knitted hat. 'That's what we play back home. Calypso.'

'Dad!' Josh kicked his ankle. 'Pack it in!'

At about ten, Ishbel pulled Josh and Nathan into the quieter bar where her friends waited, all in a row like carol singers. Janet Doinnean, the ginger woman who had made Morag Falamh so angry, introduced her husband, Father Kevin, the island's vicar. Fiona Triathan, the beautiful red-haired woman, was a doctor at the hospital and so was her tall, blond husband, Hector. Josh thought Hector was a stupid name.

'We three are that close, people take us for sisters.' Ishbel smiled at Janet and Fiona. 'When Alex was alive . . .' She glanced at Josh. 'He was my first husband, Josh . . . I did mention Alex?'

Josh nodded, awkward. 'Sort of.'

'Well, now you and your dad are here . . . I know everyone will make you welcome.'

Dr Hector smiled. 'We're fair delighted you're here, Nathan. And you're after ruining our dustbins?'

'Sorry about that.' Nathan grinned. 'But everyone thinks we're fresh out of the West Indies.'

'We are a touch behind the times.' Father Kevin rubbed a hand over his peppery hair. It looked like sheep's wool and his fingers left ridges across his skull. 'Hector's said what we all think, though. You're right welcome.'

17

Josh realised, then, how worried his dad must have been about coming to the island to live. He had hidden it, not wanting Josh to see. Now, his very best smile shone through. Everyone had to smile back at that smile. When Josh's mum had stopped smiling back, it had been the end of their marriage.

Ishbel touched Josh's arm. 'Are you all right, Josh?'

That made it the twelfth time. Island people seemed to touch each other a lot. Every time Ishbel wanted something, she would touch his arm or his face.

Josh tried to smile. 'Yeah, just tired.'

'Then away to bed with you.' She frowned. 'But first come outside with me. Mam, have you got the box ready?'

Ailsa stooped under the bar and straightened, holding a cardboard box.

'You dinna mind, Nathan?' Ishbel put her arm around Josh's shoulder. 'This is for Josh to see. Now he's the son of the house.'

Josh's dad nodded. 'I'll see you tomorrow, Josh. Have a good sleep.'

Ishbel tucked the box under her free arm and led Josh into the yard. The pub door shut behind them, blotting out the chatter, cheers from the games room, the rattle of glasses and plates. The rain had stopped and a damp breeze blew over the cobbles. Josh did not want her arm around him but he could hardly tell her to move it. It made him itch.

Ishbel glanced at Josh's face. 'I canna tell what you're thinking.'

'Well, I'm invisible in the dark. Didn't you know?' Josh felt her arm jump on his shoulder, then pull away, fast. 'I'm sorry. It was a joke.' He stared at her. 'Wow, you are white, out here! You sort of glow in the dark.'

'Something happened on the boat.'

Josh flinched. He had thought she might forget. And he should tell his dad if he was in trouble, not Ishbel.

'It was that woman, Morag.' He wanted to shut up but his mouth kept going. 'She really hated me. No one's looked at me like that, before.'

'Did she call you names, Josh?'

'No, it was the look on her face. Right evil.'

They had walked onto the crossroads. The piles of stones waited, to left and to right. Ishbel lowered her box onto the grass.

'Josh, listen to me. Morag Falamh is a wicked, dangerous woman. She canna bring herself to like good people.' Ishbel's hazel eyes glowed, wanting him to believe her. 'It's nothing to do with you being black.'

'I wasn't sure.' Josh bit his lip. 'I mean, why else would she hate me? I'd only just met her.'

'You could be green, my pet. It would make no difference.'

Now that they were talking, Josh wanted to know other things as well. 'What about the men in the big car? You didn't trust them because they were strangers, but me and dad are strangers . . .'

'You're no strangers.' She put her hands on his shoulders and, this time, he did not mind. This was not kids' stuff. 'When my husband Alex died, I doubted I'd ever be happy again. When I met your dad, it felt like a miracle. And when he told me about you . . .' She shivered. 'I'd found myself a family, all at once. You're no strangers, Josh, you're part of the island. And you're my first bairn, so I need you to help with the tolleun.'

'The stones?' He stepped back. 'No chance!'

'They're good luck, Josh. We thank the island birds by keeping the stones holy and seeing no harm comes to

19

them. No one on the island would ever hurt, kill or eat a bird.' She smiled. 'So, no turkey at Christmas. It would be like eating a friend.'

'I'll have to think about it.' Josh stepped back again. 'I mean, this is really weird. I'll have to think about it.'

'That's fine, Josh. Just watch me, this time.'

In the dim light, Ishbel scattered rice and bread over the stones. She filled a row of tin pots with fresh water, then pulled a handful of red strings from the box and tied them to the top stones. And closed her bright eyes.

'Thank you for bringing my family safe home across the sea. Look after Nathan and Josh, birds of the island. Never fly from us and leave us to our enemies. Beannachd leibh, mo cairdean.' She remembered Josh did not understand island Gaelic and translated. 'Goodbye, my friends.'

2 The Gang

The next morning, Josh sat beside Ishbel in the two-seater pony-cart, glad there was no rain, glad there was only one road to school. Ishbel's big gull flapped overhead.

'I won't get lost, anyway.'

'Goath would always find you,' Ishbel said. 'You're no worried about school?'

'Nah, easy. I'll have a gang by this afternoon.' Josh stiffened. 'Look, another tolleun.'

Ishbel had given him a map at breakfast, and he realised what the red triangles meant. The next was at Darach-burn. Sure enough, another tolleun sprouted from the grass on the far bank, across the road from the school.

'How many are there, do you know?'

'A dozen or more, Josh.' Ishbel reined the pony to a halt. 'You look that smart!' She touched his hat, his jacket, grinned at the big tongues on his trainers. 'Every lad on the island will be wanting a pair of his own. Now, off you go. Janet will take good care of you.'

'Mrs Doinnean? How's she going to take care of me?'

Ishbel laughed. 'She's your teacher, Josh.'

So far, Josh had met two doctors, a vicar and his own teacher, all friends of Ishbel. Perhaps all small islands were like this.

Ginger Janet – Mrs Doinnean – waited at the front door, still in that great jacket with all the badges. 'Come on inside, Josh. The class is waiting.'

21

Josh could tell when a group of kids had been told to behave themselves and all the faces watching him had that look. The room was split into three groups, each in a semi-circle of desks facing a blackboard. And Ishbel was wrong. The kids did think Josh was from Mars. He wondered if it was the hat. No one else was wearing a hat.

'Well, Class Three, this is Josh Williams. He and his dad have just moved into the Worm. I know you'll make him very welcome.' She patted Josh's shoulder. 'Josh, we have five classes in the school. This is the elevens to thirteens. We've found you a desk in Group Two.'

The twelve-year-olds . . . Two empty seats waited and he supposed one was for him. So, someone was off sick or late. Josh spotted the prettiest girl straight away. Finding his gang was going to be easier than he had thought. But check their clothes! Boring!

The door opened and a tall, grey-haired skeleton of a man walked in.

Janet stepped forwards. 'Mr Cashel, this—'

'I know who he is, Mrs Doinnean.' The man looked Josh over, cold-eyed, turned quickly away. 'Class Three, I have good news for you. The authorities on the mainland have decided to increase our budget next year. With any luck, we will finally have a school computer. So, our new boy might not think we are quite so primitive. That's all.' He nodded to Janet and walked out, again.

Josh snorted. 'Well, he's nice and friendly.'

'Wheesht, Josh!' Janet frowned at him. 'Mr Cashel's the school Principal. And he's quite new here himself. Now, come and meet Group Two.'

When Mrs Doinnean had finished the introductions, Josh stuck his hand up. 'Just to let you know, I'm putting my gang together today. I can't pick everyone so don't get mad if you aren't in it. I'll have a look at you in the break. That's all.'

'Aye.' Mrs Doinnean swallowed. 'I should think it is.'

For half an hour, Josh copied his new time-table into the front of his exercise books. A couple of girls were staring at him. He put his specs on upside down and both girls giggled.

At last, the bell rang and kids sprinted across the yard to the tuck shop. Josh sat on the wall next to the bicycle shed, sipping hot chocolate, waiting for the prettiest girl to walk past.

'Hey, you!'

Josh looked up. 'What?'

'What's this about a gang?' One of the girls in his group was scowling down at him.

'I'm asking people . . .' he said '. . . when I've drunk this.'

He stiffened as the prettiest girl walked past.

'You're no asking her!?'

'Look!' Josh drank the last gulp of chocolate. 'Why don't you shove off?' He stood up and had a shock. She was taller than he was.

For a start, this girl was really ugly. Frizzy pepper-coloured hair sprouted from her head into two bunches, like poodles' ears. The rest of her had hardly any hair at all – white scrappy eye-brows and lashes. Her pale little eyes squinted past a beaky nose and red blotches stained her cheeks. No, Josh thought, Poodle-ears Hamsterface isn't going to be in my gang.

She was still scowling at him. 'You'd better know my name, I suppose. I'm Triona Doinnean, Tree for short. Mrs Doinnean's my mam.'

'Never!' Josh gasped. 'You're nothing like her!'

Triona's eyes narrowed. 'Listen, you! Why're you picking Kirsty MacRath for your gang?'

'I thought she'd come in handy. To talk us out of trouble.' It was no good, Josh had to say it. 'Because she's really pretty.'

'I thought so! Well, think again, laddie! You're getting me instead.'

'No chance!'

Triona raised her big fists. 'Try and stop me!'

This was stupid. 'Look, I've got it all worked out. The prettiest girl . . .'

'Aye, to talk us out of trouble. Go on.'

Josh glared at her. 'Then the toughest boy, so no one will pick on us. But he can't be too clever . . .'

'Because you're the brains?' Triona sneered at him.

'Because it's my gang! Then I want the fittest kid. And then the richest . . .'

'Hah!' She shook her poodle-ears. 'No islander's rich. Unless you ask Morag Falamh.'

Before he could stop himself, Josh shivered. All he had to do was think about Morag's crooked mouth and her fingers on his throat and he felt sick.

'You've met her, then?' Triona stopped sneering. 'Well, if you dinna like Morag, you canna be all bad. Come on, let's find ourselves a gang.'

He stormed across the yard after her. 'It's my gang! You aren't in it!'

She ignored him. 'So, you want someone big and rough and stupid. That'll be Seoras.'

They heard Seoras Leahy before they saw him, his bellowing voice making kids flinch all around the yard.

'Hey, shrimp-face! Why's our post so late? 'Cos your auld dad canna carry it!'

A circle of kids surrounded the two boys. At Josh's old

24

school, some of them would have sided with the bully, but no one liked Seoras. Triona barged her way to the front and Josh followed.

'That's Calum Balachan, from the post office. Seoras always picks on him.'

'Yeah, he would.'

Bullies always picked on skinny, frightened kids like Calum. When Calum turned his way, brown hair on end, brown eyes blinking with terror, Josh stepped forwards.

'Hey, Seoras, pack it in! Pick on someone your own size.'

Triona grinned. 'He'll no join the gang if you talk like that.'

Seoras spun around, saw Josh and goggled, speechless.

'What's wrong, big mouth? Can't you think what to call me first?' Josh took another step forwards. 'How about fatso? How about specky-four-eyes?'

'New boy, eh?' Seoras swivelled and knocked Calum flat. 'Come on, new boy. Come and fight!'

Josh looked down at Calum Balachan. The boy's thin mouth was twitching out of control and a trickle of blood ran from his nose. But it was his clothes that did it. All Calum's things were too big for him, his sleeves rolled over his bird-bone wrists, his trouser bottoms over his sharp ankles. Josh's fists clenched and he stepped forward again. And someone walked past him, a boy Josh had not seen before. He remembered the other empty chair in Group Two and guessed that this kid usually sat in it.

'Come on, Seoras, you dinna want to fight Josh. If he sat on you, you'd squash flat.'

Tears streaming down his face, Calum scuttled out of range of Seoras's fists. Josh helped him to stand and Triona gave him a paper handkerchief.

Seoras forgot Calum, forgot Josh, his eyes swerving

towards this other boy. And Josh's brows shot up. This kid had style – great trainers, with the laces tied just right, great shirt, white with pink and yellow stripes.

'That's a serious shirt!' Josh shook his head. 'But he's in dead trouble if Seoras hits him.'

'Niall's tougher than he looks.' Triona sighed. 'Just a touch soft in the head.'

Now that Josh studied the boy, he realised that Triona was right. Niall was taller than Josh had thought and not really thin, just slim. But he was so pale he looked weaker. His hair was almost silver and his eyes pale grey.

'If you want help with your homework, Seoras, dinna hit me too hard.'

Seoras grinned. 'Man, you're a daftie, Niall! I'll hit you as hard as I fancy.'

His fists came up, ready to start thumping, and something hissed behind him, like a rattlesnake, and his fists sank back to his sides.

The scruffy girl had appeared from nowhere. Hair all over her face, she crouched, hands clawed, ready to scratch Seoras's eyes out.

'Now, I'll no fight that!' Seoras pointed at the girl angrily. 'You're a coward, Niall, waiting for Mairi to fight for you . . . Your wee shadow! Going to marry her, are you?' He laughed. 'And you'd better do that homework, mind.'

'Ach, it's a pleasure, Seoras.'

For a moment, Seoras wriggled, aching to punch Niall's calm face. He laughed again and stalked away.

Mairi felt people stare at her and shrank back, head down, as if she could melt into the floor. But Josh had seen her eyes when Seoras lifted his fists. They were wild and black.

26

'She's got no shoes.' He stared after her. 'She's as small as Calum.'

'I dinna mind being small.' Calum wiped his nose on Triona's handkerchief. 'Only sometimes, when Seoras skelps me, I wish I'd the guts to flatten him. Are you really starting a gang, Josh?'

'Mmm.' Triona was making faces behind Calum's back. Josh ignored her and walked towards Niall. 'Hey, Niall. Can you run fast?'

'I can outrun Seoras, if I have to.' Niall's brows rose. 'Why?'

'I might want you in my gang.' Josh said. 'If you can run, I mean.'

'Well, if you're thinking of timing me, I'll no bother. If you'll take my word, I just might.' Niall glanced at Triona and Calum. 'How many do you want in this gang?'

'Five.'

'And how many have you got, so far.'

'No—'

'Four.' Triona bumped Josh off his feet. 'There's Calum and you and me, Niall. And Brains, sitting on the floor, there.'

Calum swallowed. 'You canna want me, Josh?'

Oh well . . . Josh stood up. 'I suppose so.' He felt Niall smiling. 'Are you in then, Niall?'

'If Calum is.'

'I just said he is.'

'You supposed he was. So, I suppose I am.' Niall turned away. 'Come on, Calum, you'd better wash your face. You're streaky as a bacon slice.'

Josh watched the two boys walk away, one tall and pale, one skinny and undersized, still twitching. 'Nice one, Tree! You really dropped me in it! I didn't want Calum!'

Mairi appeared, like a rat out of a hole, almost under

Josh's feet. If her plaits had been less dirty, they might have been black. They looked stiff and nasty and old dirt ringed her neck.

'Mairi?' Triona frowned. 'What do you want, lass?'

Mairi opened and closed her mouth.

'She hardly ever speaks,' Triona explained. 'And if she does, it's in the Gaelic.'

'Gang,' Mairi whispered. 'Niall . . .'

Josh wished she'd stand further away. She stank. 'What?'

'Niall in gang.'

'Yeah? So what?'

'Me, too.' Her hand snapped shut on Josh's arm. 'Niall in gang. Me too!' Then she turned and ran.

'Well, so there's number five.' Triona said. 'Niall and Calum, you and me and Mairi. All the weirdos together.'

'Speak for yourself!' Josh rubbed his arm. 'But she's well weird. Those clothes!'

'Her dad died in the lifeboat and her mam right after.' Triona scowled, angrily. 'She lives with her grandad and wears her mam's auld clothes, cut down. So don't you turn your nose up at her.'

'I couldn't help it, she stinks.'

'And so you would you, living like that!'

Josh gave up. 'Look, I'm sorry, all right? Come on, I'm going back inside.'

The gang met again after lunch. At least, Josh, Calum, Niall and Triona did. Mairi watched from the other side of the yard.

'What's she staying over there for?' Josh waved to her but she shrank further into her raggy clothes.

'She's shy of you, Josh,' Calum said. 'She's shy of everyone except . . .'

28

Niall frowned down at his feet.

'. . . Except Niall.' Calum's mouth started its nervous twitching. 'Everyone knows, Niall . . .'

'Aye, they do.'

Calum took the hint and changed the subject. 'Josh, what do you eat at home with your dad?'

'It depends.' Josh thought about it. 'Fish and chips, sometimes. It depends who's cooking.'

'Fish and chips? Is that all?'

'Beans on toast? Oh.' Josh understood. 'You mean anything funny?' He lowered his voice. 'Look, don't tell anyone . . .'

Triona and Calum slid closer, mouths flapping. Niall started to smile.

'But when there's a full moon . . .' Josh lowered his voice even more. 'We take a big pot into the garden and fill it with water. And guess what we put in it?'

Calum stared at him. 'What?! What?!'

'These!' Josh grabbed a pair of noses – Calum's thin one, Triona's great beak – and twisted.

Niall fell over, laughing. Over the yard, Mairi Firinn blinked and said nothing.

After school, Josh sat on his favourite piece of wall while Niall used a felt-tip to mark everyone's homes on Ishbel's map.

'Here's Triona, in the vicarage. Then Calum, in the post office.' Niall drew a cross on each house. 'I'm further inland, next to Loch Sgailinne. And Mairi's out at Liath Bealach.'

Josh studied the map. 'Got it. OK, let's walk home.'

Triona strode next to Josh, Niall and Calum close behind. Mairi scuttled along at a safe distance behind them, their grubby shadow.

'What do your mum and dad do, Niall?' Josh walked backwards, keeping his eyes on Niall's face. 'Tree's dad the vicar and her mum's Mrs Doinnean. And Calum's mum and dad run the post office. And Mairi lives with her grandad.'

'My folk run the hospital. The two doctor Triathans.'

'Triathan!' Josh slapped himself on the head, tripped and nearly fell over Triona's feet. 'You're Doctor Hec . . . Ishbel's friends . . .'

Niall grinned. 'Dad hates "Hector", as well. I like it. Hector was a Greek hero, so it's a brave name. Like Joshua.'

Josh winced and Triona smirked at him. Niall had a way of saying things like that. Wince-making.

'Hey, where are they going?'

The big car swept past, heading towards the school.

'Probably to the coastguards for the radio.'

'Right! No telephones.' Josh frowned. 'Is there only one radio for the whole island?'

'There's six.' Triona said. 'The coastguard and light-house, the hospital and Niall's place, the post office and the Worm.'

'What about the police?'

'No police,' Triona said.

'You're joking!'

'We dinna have trouble here, Josh. If there's a problem, the Council of Islanders settles it. My mam and dad are on it with Dr Hector and Dr Fiona, the chief coastguard and the auldest man and woman. My mam's there because she's a bird warden.'

Last night, Ishbel had laughed when Josh tried to find a key to the pub door. Islanders never locked their houses. They wouldn't last ten minutes in London.

'What's a bird warden for? To protect the birds?'

30

'We're an important nesting site, Josh. And we've got Radcliffe's Tern.' Triona grinned at him. 'You look that interested! But Radcliffe's Tern are special. They're really rare. No one knows where they nest, but they fish around the coast.'

They had reached the church grounds and Triona stopped at the gate in the wall.

'This is my place. Come up and see the view.'

A steep path wound between the tombstones and Josh wondered if Triona ever got scared, walking there in the dark. Then the path twisted steeper and he concentrated on keeping up with her big feet.

'Mairi's following. I thought she'd stay on the road, she's that superstitious. She prefers animals to people, apart from . . .' Triona pulled a face. 'Sorry, Niall.'

Niall just shrugged but Josh could see that it bothered him. Everyone on the island must know that Mairi Firinn loved him.

Calum prodded Josh's back. 'Josh, what's yellow and swings from tree to tree?'

Josh stared at him. 'What?'

Calum giggled. 'Tarzipan!'

Josh's mouth fell open. He had just heard the oldest joke in the world.

Triona groaned. 'Ach, Calum! Don't be starting on that again! Josh, stand here and look back.' She pointed back down the path. 'See, we're the highest point in the town.'

Josh stared over the low, black and brown roofs, along the ferry pier and into the eye-shaped harbour. Seals to the east, lighthouse to the west. And the gap in the cliffs, like a magic door into the ocean. The breeze tasted of the sea. He wanted to fill his lungs with it, clean all the grot away.

'I wish I'd brought my camera. I'd send photos . . .' He stopped.

'Who to?' Triona nudged him. 'All your London friends?'

'Yeah. I suppose.'

'And your mam? Your other one?' Triona nudged him again, then jumped back at the look on his face. 'What's wrong with that? Everyone knows . . .'

'Well, everyone can shut up about it, all right?' Josh bit his lip. 'Look, if Mairi's got to walk to Liath Bealach, we'd better get moving. See you tomorrow, Tree.'

'You might and you might not. Telling me to shut up . . .' Triona stomped away from the main path, down a row of steps to the vicarage. 'What's that on the door?' She walked faster, trying to see. And stopped. 'Ach . . . no . . .'

3   Crow's Head

Triona staggered backwards, hands clenched over her mouth.

'What?' Josh hurried towards her. 'Ugh! What's that?'

'It's a crow's head.'

'A real . . . ? You mean that's . . . ?' Josh swallowed. 'That's gross!'

Nailed to the middle of the door, the black bird-head looked very dead, stiff-feathered, dull-eyed, beak gaping too wide.

Triona's face crumpled. 'It's a curse on us! Who'd have done it?'

'Morag was right mad with your mum, yesterday. She said she'd be sorry.' Josh shuddered. 'That's gross! Really gross.'

Someone had killed the bird, cut its head off, nailed it to the wood.

'Ach, it's more than gross. It's evil!' Calum hardly dared to look. 'If Morag Falamh did that, she's as bad as my mam says.'

'She's worse.' Now that Josh was talking, he felt better. He could look at the bird's head and talk and feel his new friends around him. He was fine. He was OK. 'She nearly pushed me off the ferry. She really had it in for me.'

'Someone take it down! Take it away!' Triona sobbed, helplessly. 'Niall? Josh?'

'I'll do it.' Josh took a deep breath. 'I'm the Boss, remember. I do things like this.'

'If you want to, Josh, you're welcome.' Niall put his arm around Triona's shoulders. 'Wheesht, lass! The bad luck's on whoever did it, not on your mam and dad.'

'I told you, Morag did it.' Josh's fingers hovered, not wanting to touch the bits with blood. Splinters of bone glittered in the broken neck. 'Yug! This is awful. Hey!'

Mairi tore past him, skidding into the door. She screamed something in Gaelic, went on screaming.

'Mairi, your grandad will know what to do.' Niall tried to calm both girls at once. Triona snorting and sobbing into his right shoulder, Mairi cursing at his left. 'He'll put the poor, wee thing to rest.'

Josh blinked. 'Look, I know this is a sick thing to do. But it's only a bird, right? It's not murder or anything.'

'Josh . . .' Niall shook his pale head. 'Josh, you dinna understand. On the island, to kill a bird is worse than murder. It's unholy.'

'Oh, come off it! You don't believe that?'

No one answered. Josh realised he had just made a big, big mistake. He had to do something. He grabbed the crow's head and pulled.

Flying high, low . . . Swoop down . . . Yeeee!!! Cool air. Happy, happy . . .

Josh gasped. 'What's happening? Niall . . .?'

Far away, Niall's voice. 'Dinna worry, Josh, we're with you.'

Wheee!! Down to the tree . . . Hup! Ah, that's grand . . . What's this? Bacon fat! Thank you! Like bacon fat. Hop down, beak open, let's have it . . .

Snap. Josh felt it. A snap as a trap shut on his leg. Bones breaking. Pain . . . He blinked upwards, eyes funny, not seeing right. A hand in a thick, leather glove reached for him. Huge hand. And a knife in it . . . Sharp, silver-glittery knife . . .

'Ahhh!' Josh stumbled backwards, clutching his throat. 'Ugh . . . Oh yuk! . . . Horrible.'

'It's over.' Niall trembled, white to the lips. 'Ach, that was truly horrendous! Tree, are you fine to stand on your own? I have to be sick.'

Triona nodded and Niall staggered to the nearest patch of flower-bed, dropped to his knees and threw up.

'That didn't happen,' Josh said. 'It didn't.'

'We all felt the poor wee thing die.' Triona shivered. 'Mairi, take it to your grandad. Maybe he can stop the bad luck hitting us.'

Mairi ripped the bird's head free and big, dirty tears ran down her face. For a moment, she gazed into Josh's eyes and he thought he read her mind. Stupid. But he thought she nodded and said, 'You're one of us, now.' She clutched the crow's head to her chest and ran down the church path and away.

The post office was only three minutes from Triona's place but the boys needed more time than that before they could speak to each other. They walked as slowly as they could.

Josh finally cleared his throat. 'OK. Does that sort of thing happen a lot, around here?'

'Not crow's heads, Josh. But there's magic here.' Niall glanced at Josh's face. 'Did Morag really attack you?'

'She went crazy . . . Oh!' Josh remembered. 'Oh, right! The birds flew at her and I ran off.'

'Then they knew you were part of the island, before you even got here,' Calum said. 'Because you're Ishbel's family . . . Eh, Niall?'

'It sounds right enough. But I'm worried about Morag going for Josh like that.'

35

'*You're* worried!' Josh spluttered. 'I nearly wet myself!'

They all managed a shaky laugh, then a proper laugh, then a fit of giggles. Calum stopped at the post office door. 'Come in, why don't you? Come and meet my mam and dad.'

Josh nodded. 'Great.'

Josh remembered Seoras in the playground, teasing Calum because his dad was old. Now he saw that it was true. Both Balachans were grey-haired, old-fashioned looking. They must have been old when Calum was born.

Mr Balachan's face crinkled in a shy smile. His voice was deafening. 'Calum, this is nice! Your friends coming in!'

'Have you eaten, any of you?' Mrs Balachan asked. 'There's scones, if you're hungry?'

'I'd better not.' Josh watched the two old people shuffle closer together, pleased and embarrassed at the same time that Calum's friends had taken the trouble to call. He realised that they were very deaf.

'Josh has started a gang!' Calum yelled. 'And I'm in it!'

'You're in it?' Mr Balachan said. 'Are you really? Did you hear that, mam? Calum's in a gang!'

He sounded surprised, Josh thought.

'Of course he is!' Josh bawled. 'I only picked the best . . .' He gave Calum his biggest, ear-to-ear grin. 'So Calum had to be in it!' It hurt his throat to shout so hard. 'See you tomorrow, Calum!'

'Oh, aye. I'll wait for you, if you like?'

Calum looked so eager, Josh felt sorry for him. 'Great! I'll see you! Bye, Mr Balachan . . . Mrs Balachan . . .'

As the door shut, Josh met Niall's grey eyes. 'I've knackered my throat.'

'It was a nice thing to say, though, about picking the best.'

36

'Well . . .' Josh shrugged. 'I bet he doesn't take many people home.'

'It's won you two friends, anyway.' Niall started to walk, quickly. 'Calum and me.'

Josh followed him. 'Niall? Where'd you get that shirt? It's really smart.'

Niall's eyes glittered. 'I saw you looking at it. My mam's brother designs clothes. He's always sending me things. I sometimes model for him – you know, kids' stuff for him to show around.'

'Got any pictures?'

'One or two.' Niall slowed down, again. 'Josh, will you tell me something? Why did you really pick us? Calum and Mairi and Tree and me?'

'You sort of picked yourselves.' Josh had discovered something. He couldn't lie to Niall. 'You don't mind, do you?'

'Ach, no. I just wondered. Who did you want, instead of me?'

Josh groaned. 'If you really want to know . . . I thought about Seoras.'

'Did you now? You'd have lost Mairi and Calum, if you'd got Seoras.' He smiled. 'And Triona canna stand the lad. Aren't you glad you never asked him, Josh?'

'Funny!' Josh glared at him. 'You think you're really clever, don't you?'

Niall shrugged. 'I am clever. But I like you, Josh, and I'm glad you're the Boss. You'll be even better than you think you will.' They had reached the bridge over Sgail-inburn. 'Shall I wait for you, tomorrow?'

'Yeah, why not? We walking or cycling?'

'You're the Boss. But Calum's no got a bike.'

Josh sighed. 'Walking, then. And I bet Mairi hasn't got

one, either? Why don't you cycle to school, so she can't keep up with you?'

Niall stopped walking. 'She hasn't any shoes, either. I could walk on glass, couldn't I? That would stop her in a hurry.'

'Hey, come on . . .' Josh looked at Niall's stiff, hurt face. 'I thought you hated her following you.'

'I do.' Niall groaned and kicked the bridge. 'Ach, I'm sorry! I keep feeling that poor bird die. And I'm never sure what I think about Mairi. I'll see you tomorrow.'

Josh watched him walk along the left fork of the crossroads, out of sight behind a mound of brambles. That was something else for Josh to think about . . . Niall and Mairi.

'He never did!' Ishbel's voice, in the kitchen.

'He did!'

'Right out, in front of everyone? He really said that?'

Josh walked through the door, ears twitching, to find Ishbel and Janet Doinnean falling off their chairs laughing. When they saw him, they gulped and turned bright red.

'Hello there, Josh.' Ishbel hurried towards him and kissed his chin. 'Did you have a fine first day at school?'

'It was OK. I got the gang together, anyway.'

'Aye, I heard. Who did you get, exactly?'

Josh glared at Janet's ginger hair. 'Hasn't she told you?'

'Not yet, no.' Ishbel grinned at him. 'Come on, Josh.'

'OK. There's Niall and Triona . . .'

'My Triona?' Janet goggled. 'Well, good luck to you, Josh.'

'And there's Calum and Mairi.'

'Mairi Firinn?'

'Why not?' Josh snapped. 'I can have anyone I want.'

'Aye, aye, pet. I was just surprised about Mairi . . .'

Then Ishbel nodded. 'Ach, of course! She'd follow Niall to the island's end, if he asked her.'

Josh might have said something but Ailsa appeared, backing out of the pantry with a tray in her hands. Bits of cake-mix spotted her glasses.

'I thought I heard you, lad. Now, sit yourself down and let's get tea and shorties into you.'

'Great.' Josh kicked his bag under the table. 'That looks great.'

His dad appeared from the hallway. 'Hi there . . .'

'Dad, come and look at this.'

'I could smell it from the bar.' Nathan grinned. 'And you look as happy as a new angel in heaven, boy. Had a good day at school?'

Josh nodded, eyes on the tray of biscuits.

Ailsa took his hat off and kissed the top of his head. 'And why wouldn't he? This is his home, now. He's going to be very happy.' She tipped an avalanche of biscuits onto Josh's plate. 'Now, you try those, my lad, and dinna say you've tasted better.'

Josh nodded, again. He had never seen his dad so happy. Just for the moment, he could forget about the crow's head on the vicarage door and Mairi Firinn screaming and Calum's old, deaf parents. And Niall, who was a bit odd. And Triona who looked tough but cried like a baby because she was scared of bad luck. He bit the first buttery biscuit and grinned. He had his gang and his dad was happy. Everything would be just fine.

After Thursday breakfast, Josh gathered the last slices from the previous day's loaves and carried them outside. That was another island custom, to give the birds the last of everything.

'Come on, birds.' He shredded the crusts onto the grass. 'Come on, I can see you.'

Birds hopped along the pub roof, waiting.

'All right, suit your . . . Yoi!' A bird flapped into his face. 'Hey! Mind the hat!'

It scrabbled for a grip on his jumper, wings beating his chin.

'Stand still, Josh. You're frightening her.' Ishbel watched him from the kitchen door. 'Stand still now.'

Josh stood still and the small gull flapped twice then settled down, blinking yellow eyes.

'Josh . . .' Ishbel laughed. 'I think she's your bird.'

It sounded so stupid, Josh snorted and the bird squealed at him.

'You should be proud to have her.' Ishbel sighed. 'I know it's difficult to understand.'

Josh grunted and the bird flopped down to join the mass of feather and beak squabbling on the grass. 'It's weird. Everything about this place is weird.'

Josh had crossed the yard when he remembered he had not told Ishbel about the crow's head.

Niall waited at the Sgailinburn bridge, swinging his feet over the wooden fence. The sun turned his hair silver. And he wore another of his uncle's shirts, blue and green. Real style. 'It's a fine, soft day, Josh. The air's sweet as honey.'

'Smells like old mud to me.'

'And you're in a grand mood! Let's walk and I'll cheer you up.' He started to whistle a fast, spiky rhythm.

Not bad, Josh thought. 'Is that Scottish?'

'It's like the island, a bit of Scottish, Irish, old Celtic. We're a mixture of blood. I take after the Viking islanders.'

Josh fell into step with him. 'Where's Mairi?'

'Behind us. She tries to hide sometimes.'

Yesterday, Josh might have said something about that. Today, he liked walking and whistling with Niall too much to spoil it. Josh had to admit, Niall was a great whistler.

Calum popped out of the post office door. 'It's a fine day, Josh.'

Josh nodded. 'Grand. Fine.' He glanced at Niall. 'The air's like honey.'

Calum laughed, then trotted faster. 'What's green and red and goes round and round?'

'Don't tell me!'

'A frog in a food mixer!'

'Calum!' Josh groaned. 'You're as bad as my dad!'

Three minutes later, Triona met them at the church path, pretending it was an accident but walking with them, whistling as well. All the gang together. Josh glanced around, hoping people would notice, and saw a statue at the other side of the road. And a big, black bird craning around it to stare at him. He rubbed his eyes with his fists, hurting himself. The bird vanished.

'Tree, what's that statue for?'

'It's the monument to the lost lifeboat.' Tree's white brows frowned. 'Did Ishbel no tell you? Her husband died in it.'

Josh's hands turned cold. He knew that Ishbel's first husband, Alex Ros, had been Ailsa's son. So, Ishbel was really Ailsa's daughter-in-law. He walked to the bronze statue – a lifeboat man with metal arms raised for help. Under its feet, a plaque listed the names of the dead.

'Alex Ros,' Josh read. 'Ishbel's husband, Ailsa's son.' He peered closer. 'Liam Balachan . . .'

'My uncle,' Calum said.

Josh had to keep reading. 'Ryan Triathan . . . Alasdair Triathan . . .'

'My cousins,' Niall said. 'Pol Doinnean was Father Kevin's brother. And Tormod Firinn was Mairi's dad.'

'Ishbel never told me. I thought Mr Ros must have died of something like cancer . . . or a car crash.' Josh shivered. 'What happened?'

'The birds warned us, Josh,' Niall said. 'A ship was in trouble and the lifeboat got ready to sail. But Fearchas swore the birds wanted the boat to stay home. The ship was already lost, so there was no point in risking the storm. But you canna tell coastguards something like that.'

Josh gazed at the bronze man. He felt dizzy, scared. 'So they went out in the storm?'

'Aye, and drowned . . . Alex Ros, my cousins, Mairi's dad, everyone.' Niall pressed his fist onto the stone and his knuckles shone white. 'Mairi's mam died straight after and Fearchas shut himself away. It was a horrible thing, Josh.'

Seoras waited at the school gates. 'What a grand gang you've got, Josh! Niall and Triona . . . And shrimp-face Balachan! And Mairi Firinn!'

Josh looked Seoras up and down. 'Better them than you, dog-breath.'

'Is that right?' Seoras grinned. 'No one else would join you, that's the truth of it. You dinna belong here. You're an outsider. No one wants you.'

Josh stared at the cruel, laughing face and the same feeling he'd shivered at near the monument came back. First, that bird being there again. And then people dying, thinking birds could have saved them. The islanders were different. Maybe Seoras was right.

'Josh is no outsider, Seoras,' Niall said. 'He's Ishbel's family and he's our friend.'

And the seagull from the Worm flopped down Josh's face, a squawking tangle of wing and webbed claw, its tail up his nose, its feathers in his mouth. It rammed its backside in his face then dropped, squealing, onto his shoulder.

Seoras stopped laughing.

'See that, Seoras? Would an island bird set on an outsider?' Triona thumped Josh on the back. 'The birds know Josh is one of us.'

To Josh's amazement, Seoras nodded. He did not look too happy about it, but he nodded.

After that, none of the other kids gave Josh funny looks. A bird had sat on him, so they thought he was OK. Weird. They ran to look at his seagull, all smiling, pleased for him. It pooped down his jumper, which Calum said was good luck. Just before the bell rang, it stretched its white neck, wiggled its tail and thought about flying off.

'Bird.' Mairi squeezed to Josh's side. 'Josh bird!'

'Mairi, Josh needs a name for it,' Niall said. 'You'll have to help him, he doesn't have the Gaelic yet.'

Clever, Josh thought. Mairi's face did not change but her dark eyes glittered. She would do anything for Niall, Josh decided. Absolutely anything.

'Ow!' Josh glared at the bird. 'It's got claws like razors!'

'Na spogan,' Mairi said. 'Claws.'

'Spogan's a bit . . . Spog!' Josh grinned. 'Spog's OK. For an ugly bird like this.'

Spog shook herself and tried to nip Josh's nose, then flapped up and away.

At first break, the gang spread along their wall to talk. Josh took a deep breath . . . and sneezed. Mairi had slithered next to him. She stank. He took a smaller breath.

43

'Listen, I've been thinking. We know who put the crow's head on the door, right?'

'We have no proof,' Niall said. 'None at all.'

Josh ignored him. 'These men are sniffing around . . . and it's our island, right?'

Niall sighed. 'Go on, Josh. It's our island.'

'So, we've got to find out what's happening.'

Triona nodded. 'What are they looking for? And why stay at Falamh Taigh with Morag?'

'Their mail comes by special boat, all sealed up in sacks,' Calum said. 'We dinna know their names, even.'

Josh rubbed his specs up and down his nose. 'The mail's all sealed up, Calum?'

'Aye. Metal bands around the sacks.' Calum's mouth twitched and he held it still with his thumb. 'But I could pull them off and take a wee peek inside.'

'Would you?'

'I dinna see why not.' Calum thought about it. 'My dad would box my ears if he caught me, mind, but I could try. And put the bands back on with pliers.'

Josh stared at him. 'You ever done that before?'

'Ach, no. But there's always a first time.' Calum suddenly grinned. 'Dinna look so worried, Josh, I'll no get caught.'

Josh forgot and took another deep breath. This time, he choked. 'Look, Mairi, if you're going to be in the gang, you can start washing! Haven't you heard of soap?'

Her face crumpled like wet paper. She jumped up, gulped and let the tears run down her face. Then she spun on her heel and ran.

'Ach, well done, Josh!' Niall shook his head. 'You know she lives on her own with auld Fearchas. I doubt they've a bar of soap between them.'

Triona's eyes narrowed. 'You've a big mouth on you, Josh. It's no wonder your mam ran off.'

'Triona!' Calum pulled a face. 'That's no fair . . .'

Josh sat very still. That had really hurt. He wondered if he was going to cry. 'No, Tree's right. I shouldn't have said that . . . My mam ran off with Carl Benjamin.'

'Who's Carl Benjamin?'

'You're joking!' Josh gawped at the three, blank faces. 'You don't know who Carl Benjamin is? He's lead singer with Timelapse! Don't you listen to pop music, out here?'

Triona shrugged. 'We like our own music.'

'But Carl's famous . . . It was in all the papers!' Josh still remembered it so clearly. 'We kept seeing her on television. And in the papers – Sexy Steena Leaves Family for Rock Idol. It was awful.'

No one knew what to say. Maybe they were too embarrassed to speak to him? Then Niall touched Josh's arm.

'A while back . . .' He looked down. 'My mam and dad weren't always happy, Josh. I can remember how it felt, as if it was my fault.'

'I've never talked about it, not even to Dad.' Josh met Niall's eyes. 'Reporters followed me to school and asked me to send Mum a message. I wouldn't but they printed my photograph and made it all up, anyway . . . Abandoned Son Appeals to Rock Star. Send my Mummy Home. I never called her mummy!'

'What will you do about Mairi?'

'I'll say I'm sorry.' Josh nodded. 'I'll ask Ishbel to take me to Mairi's place after school.'

4 Something Nasty

Ishbel took Josh to Liath Bealach in the two-seater pony trap. She was not happy and she made him do his homework first, then Ailsa insisted that they all sat down and ate. Josh had his first taste of his gran's speciality – mealie pudding – a sort of stuffing sausage. Really good stuff. Then he had pub work to do, filling dishes with peanuts and crisps and helping his dad roll beer kegs from the cellar. Finally, Ishbel sat next to him in the trap. She handed him a plastic carrier bag.

'What's this?'

Bottles of shampoo and bars of soap filled the bag to bursting. Josh swallowed and glanced at Ishbel's face. She would not smile at him.

'Ishbel, I'm sorry I upset Mairi. Me and my big mouth! I'll make it up to her. Honest.'

'Then that's all right.' She clicked her tongue and the pony started forwards. 'But I canna say I look forward to meeting Fearchas.'

Josh bit his lip. 'Niall told me about the lifeboat.'

'Aye. Five years past.' Ishbel sighed. 'Fearchas came to the men's funeral and screamed at us all . . . "This is your fault! The birds never lie to us." I've no seen him since.'

No wonder she was not smiling.

'If you really don't want to come. I could drive myself.'

Ishbel relaxed and sat further back, hands playing with

the reins. 'No, Josh, I'll take you. If you can be brave and face Mairi, I can be brave and face Fearchas.'

The pony took the right fork at the crossroads, climbing past Niall's house. Over the roof, Loch Sgailinne glinted a dull grey and swans floated on it, like clouds.

Ishbel smiled. 'If we're lucky, we might see the eagles. They're a brave sight.'

The road wound over moorland grasses, heather and gorse – every shade of purple carpet, yellow and brown velvet, grey rocks, long views dotted with dusty-white sheep. Every so often the pony passed a bundle of something, sitting at the roadside.

'What's that?' Josh pointed to a rope-bound package.

'That's island cloth. The crofters make it.'

'What . . . ? From wool and stuff?'

Ishbel nodded. 'First, shear your sheep. Then dye the wool with crotal over a peat fire . . .'

'What's crotal?'

'Josh!' She sighed. 'Ach, you dinna know much about us, do you?'

'Not yet. I'm trying, though.'

Ishbel's face softened. 'Aye, of course you are. Crotal dye is from lichens. After the wool is dyed, it's carded free of tangles, spun into thread and woven on hand-looms. That's how a lot of folk make their livings here.'

Josh remembered what he had thought, on the ferry. This really was a documentary about Primitive Life. But did he still think this was Grot Island? He was not sure.

Further to the west, the land turned into peat bogs. Between peat and moorland, more water glinted, a mini-sea stretching half-way to the horizon.

'I forgot my map,' Josh said. 'What's that?'

'Loch Darach. The only loch we dinna swim in. It's unlucky and the island on it's unluckier . . .' Ishbel lowered her voice. 'Folk say fairies live on Eilean Sithiche.'

'Oh yeah?'

'Aye, truly. Now, here's the start of Beinn Dubh. There's a fairy thorn tree up on the summit. We should go up there, it's good luck.'

Josh rolled his eyes. 'But the fairy island is bad luck?'

'Ach, I know it's confusing . . .' Ishbel frowned. 'And poor Mairi walks this way, twice a day.'

The pony trotted along the road for twenty minutes, the valley slowly deepening, growing darker and wilder. More sheep grazed here and Josh wondered what it would be like in winter. Would Mairi trudge through snow to school? Ishbel teased the reins and the pony slowed.

'There's the croft.' She pointed ahead. 'The roof is thatch over turf and the walls are tarred for extra water-proofing.'

Josh stared at the low, black-walled building. Ropes and stones held the thatch down and blue smoke oozed through. It gave the place a floaty, misty look.

'There's no chimney. It must be like a kipper factory in there!'

'It's peat smoke,' Ishbel said. 'No so bad, once you're used to it. That shed around the back is where Fearchas does his weaving. He makes right fine cloth, Fearchas Firinn.'

Before the trap could reach the front door, it creaked open and Fearchas Firinn appeared. Josh knew that Fearchas was seventy – Ishbel had told him – and he had not expected such a tall powerful old man.

'He looks like a Red Indian!' Josh whispered. 'Look at that hat!'

Above the hooked nose and white mane of hair, Fearchas wore a bowler hat with a gull's feather in it. A real gull perched on his left shoulder, something like a starling on his right.

'He cares for sick animals,' Ishbel said. 'He'd have made a grand vet.'

Fearchas cracked his knuckles, then pulled an ancient brown pipe from his pocket and stuck it, unlit, into his mouth.

'I'll speak the Gaelic to him, Josh. Just stay quiet, now.' Ishbel hopped down from the cart and Josh followed.

'Ciamar a tha thu, Fearchas?'

For a good ten minutes, Ishbel talked and Fearchas refused to answer. The man's black eyes flickered when she mentioned Alex, her dead husband. Then she mentioned Mairi and the pipe flipped from one side of his mouth to the other. He said something back, a long stream of Gaelic.

'Josh, he can understand English. Say what you want and we'll get away from here.' Ishbel's hazel eyes shone too bright, as if she needed to cry. 'He's a cruel, heartless auld man!'

Josh gripped the plastic carrier and walked forwards. 'Mr Firinn, I came to say sorry to Mairi. And I want to invite her home with me, tomorrow, after school.' He glanced at Ishbel. 'That's all right, isn't it? I'll ask the whole gang . . . It's Friday, so there's the weekend for homework.'

'It's fine by me, Josh.'

Josh turned back to Fearchas. 'Can I talk to her?'

Nothing.

'I have to say I'm sorry. I'm the Boss. I shouldn't make the others cry.'

Nothing.

Josh had an idea. 'That crow's head was horrible. We all know who did it. I mean, it had to be her.'

The pipe moved.

'She doesn't like me much . . . Morag Falamh.'

Ishbel touched his arm. 'Josh, what have you not been telling me?'

'I didn't want you and dad to worry. But she tried to throw me off the boat. And nailed a crow's head to the vicarage door.'

'So, you're the Dark Outsider.' Fearchas had a good voice for the Gaelic but it sounded strange speaking English. 'If you're just here and she's just back, you'd have been on the same ferry. I doubt she was happy to see you.'

'She started talking rubbish.'

'What rubbish?' Fearchas strode towards him. 'Can you remember what she said, laddie?'

Josh blinked. 'Not really. Something about me being too late.'

'Ach, then it is the time! Who's in this gang of yours?'

'Well, Mairi and me . . . Calum Balachan . . . Triona Dionnean . . .' Josh hesitated, not sure if Fearchas knew about Mairi and Niall. 'And Niall Triathan.'

'The Lone Children.' Fearchas closed his eyes. 'It all comes true. And you are late, laddie. There's only a week before next Thursday.'

'What's next Thursday?'

'Strange that your Triathan has the Viking looks. I dinna suppose it matters, but it's a strange thing. What do you think of Niall Triathan?'

Josh knew he had to say whatever came into his head. Fearchas would see a lie. And what came into his head surprised him. 'Oh. I'm frightened for him.'

Fearchas nodded, slowly. 'Then you're the right one to be leading them. Be careful of Morag Falamh. She's no witch, but there's that much hate in her, it could give her power to destroy, if she finds the right words. Other

Falamhs have tried magic, before now. Their loch's cursed for it.' He turned away. 'Take care of your friends, Joshua Williams. That's what you're here to do.'

Josh tried again. 'Ishbel, what's next Thursday?'

But Ishbel stared after Fearchas. And then Mairi slid outside, looking even more like a little, wild animal. Her dark eyes glittered.

'Mairi, I came to say I'm sorry. It's not your fault if you haven't got any soap . . .' Josh gave her the bag. 'The gang's coming to the Worm tomorrow and we're swimming . . .'

Mairi frowned. 'Niall?'

'I haven't asked him, yet, but he's bound to come. I mean, there's nothing else to do around here.'

Ishbel laughed. 'Josh!'

'Well, there isn't. Anyway, *I* want you to come.'

Mairi looked doubtful and Ishbel stepped forwards. 'You can borrow one of my auld costumes, Mairi. And we've plenty of towels . . .'

Mairi peered into the bag. Then she nodded and ran back into the house, closing the door behind her.

'Well, so that's that.' Ishbel wrapped her arms around Josh's ribs and hugged him. 'Ahh! You're a grand lad. And if you're having your friends swimming, you take good care of them.'

"Course I will.' Josh hopped back into the cart. 'What were you and Fearchas talking about?'

'The lifeboat going down.' Ishbel took the pony forwards at a smart trot. 'He made me very angry.'

'Yeah, I noticed.'

'He said the real killer was our men's pride.' Ishbel shivered. 'That hurt me, Josh, to think of Alex dying because he was afraid to look afraid. They were all brave men.'

51

'Do you still miss him?' Josh looked at her. 'After five years?'

'Aye. Like you miss your mam, I expect.'

'No.' Startled, Josh realised that that was true. He shook his head. 'I think I'm glad she went off. She was never happy, whatever Dad did.' He remembered all the nasty words, all the times his mum had glared at him as if she hated him for being fat and clumsy and spectacled. But, most of all, he remembered her always complaining, always jealous of people in the news. 'We were never rich or famous enough for her. She wanted to be a star.'

Ishbel patted his knee. 'Well, Josh, you're famous enough for me.'

Josh grinned, pleased with himself for coming to the island and for saying sorry to Mairi, liking Ishbel for always telling him the truth about things. Then he heard something. The pony's head jerked up and her grey ears flattened.

'What's wrong, pet?' Ishbel clicked her tongue, gently. 'Liath, what's wrong?'

'I heard something.' Josh peered back over his shoulder at the undulating heather. 'Somewhere over there.'

The sky had darkened slightly. In another hour, it would be night black.

Ishbel shook her head. 'I canna see anything. Was it coming from Loch Darach?'

'Do you think it's fairies?' Josh giggled. 'It wasn't all that—'

Liath's head jerked, again, and her hooves banged faster on the road.

'Gently! Gently, now.' Ishbel eased back on the reins. 'Josh, can you see anything?'

'It sounded like an animal.' He swallowed and met

Ishbel's wide eyes. 'You haven't got something nasty on the island, have you?'

'Nothing at all. Ach!' She pulled back on the reins. 'Look up there! They know something, those birds.'

Far overhead, a pair of cross-shaped silhouettes spiralled and swooped. Their lonely cries did sound like warnings.

'Wow!' Josh stood up. 'They're really something! What are they?'

'Golden eagles. Josh, sit down, quickly now.' Ishbel flipped the reins. 'Liath, walk on. Walk!' She put her hand on Josh's elbow, making him look at her. 'Now, dinna be frightened, Josh. Liath can out-run anything we'll meet out here. But keep looking back, I'll keep my eyes on the road.'

'Like riding shotgun.' His toes curled in his shoes. 'Is something following us?'

'I canna be sure. But my hair's bristling like an old dog's.'

In the gloom behind them, something pushed between rough gorse, bounded over tussocks of grass. Josh clung to the seat as Liath broke into a scuttling trot.

'Can you see something, Josh?'

'Shadows.'

They both heard it, this time. A low, rattling snarl echoed down the road.

'A cat!' Ishbel gasped. 'God save us, it sounds like a wildcat.'

'But there aren't any cats on the island!'

'I know that. But my ears know a cat when they hear one. Hold tight, Josh. Liath! Hup! Hup!'

The pony stretched her neck and clattered past Niall's house, Josh wishing there had been a turn-off so he could run to Doctor Hector and ask for . . . what? A shotgun? He hung on as the trap rattled and skidded down the hill.

The hotel lights gleamed ahead, bouncing from side to side. Heart thudding, Josh risked another backwards glance.

Two red sparks leapt onto the road. A dark shape swirled around them, creeping along, breathing. He swore he could hear it breathing.

Ishbel opened her mouth and started to sing at the top of her voice. Gaelic. Josh had no idea what she was singing but he joined in with his favourite Challenger single, 'Traffic jams, on the moo-oove . . .' He hoped the red eyes liked Challenger. Before he could find out, the trap spun sideways, over the crossroads and into the cobbled yard and nearly through the wall into the front bar. Ishbel hauled Liath in a tight circle, steering her into the yellow glow of the windows. The pony stopped, trembling, foam dripping from her neck and sides.

Ishbel dropped the reins. 'You saw something, Josh. What did you see?'

'Eyes.' Josh swallowed. 'Red eyes.'

'Dinna tell your dad, Josh. Not until we find out what it is.'

'No.'

Ishbel put her arms around him, again. This time, he hugged her back. His knees shook against the wooden seat.

'You're a good, brave lad, Josh. And something's happening and Fearchas Firinn knows. And it's about that gang of yours.'

Josh closed his eyes. He had had one good day here. And now he was scared.

Josh mumbled awake at seven o'clock the next morning, dreaming that something pecked his window. Half-asleep, he hauled it open. A small, white gull thrust her beak into his face.

'Spog!' Josh shooed the bird away but she ducked under his hands, squawking. 'You greedy guts! Go on, get lost.'

Spog would not get lost and Josh gave up, searching the room for food. All he found was his emergency bag of crisps. He emptied it out of the window and she pounced like a white vulture.

Josh needed to talk to Ishbel about last night but his dad kept getting in the way. When Nathan Williams was happy, he wanted to make everyone else happy and that meant juggling scones or telling bad jokes or doing one of his funny walks around the kitchen. Spluttering with laughter, Josh had to wait until Ishbel kissed him goodbye.

'It wasn't a dream, was it?'

'No, lad. So look after yourself.' She saw Nathan frown and added. 'The birds are circling the harbour. A fine storm's brewing.'

'I hope it waits until we've swum.'

Clomping over the cobbles, Josh thought Niall had forgotten him. He was surprised by how much he wanted Niall to be waiting. 'Niall?' Unless he was hiding?

'I'm over here.'

Josh peered across the road. 'Where?'

'Here.' Niall walked forwards on his knees. 'By the tolleun.'

The tolleun next to the bridge had toppled, stones and old bone and Ishbel's decorations scattered over the grass.

'Shoot!' Josh whistled. 'What did that? A car?'

'No skid marks. Now help me put it back up.' Niall shuddered. 'This is desperate bad luck.'

Josh dropped his haversack and started to toss stones back on the heap. 'You reckon it was deliberate?'

'Look at the way it fell, Josh. To the south, as if

something hit it from the north.' Niall frowned. 'And there's funny wee scratches in the stones.'

'There's what?' Josh snatched the stone from Niall's hand. 'Cat scratches!'

'Cat scratches?' Niall's brows shot into his blond fringe. 'Ach, that's impossible.'

'Ishbel took me to Mairi's, last night, and something chased us. It sounded like a cat.'

'Well, a cat's no done that.' Niall stood up. 'It would take a grand lot of ginger tom to knock this thing over.'

'Niall!' Josh stood up as well. 'I heard it! It's fine when you talk about birds. But when I hear a cat, I'm nuts, right?'

'Josh, there are no cats on the island.'

They held a stone each and, angry with each other, slammed them onto the tolleun. Ripples of energy swarmed through their fingers, up from the heart of the stone pile.

'Oh-oh . . .' Josh groaned. 'Oh great! Niall, it's starting, again.'

'It's all right, Josh. Just let it happen.'

And they were flying high, surrounded by boiling, black cloud. Sparks of electricity spluttered in the darkness. Cold energy. Green energy. Horrible, sick green.

'Cat.' A voice rumbled and sparked around them. 'Poison cat.'

The dark clouds melted and the island lay below them, rotting. Concrete bunkers studded the valleys and the mountains smouldered, scorched to the bare rock. Roncamas had crumbled, the buildings in ruins, the pier broken and stained with rust. But the worst thing was the sea. All around the island, the water glistened with spilt oil, yellow foam and the silvery bellies of dead fish.

5 Dark Waters

Josh opened his eyes. He still stood, right hand glued to the tolleun, Niall blinking at the other side.

'You OK?'

'I think so. Ach, that was grotesque! As if the island had died.' Niall shivered. 'Did you hear the voice?'

'"Poison cat." Makes a lot of sense, that does.' Josh unpeeled his hand, finger by finger, from the lump of rock. 'Do you believe me about the cat now?'

'I have to. So, that's a worry, isn't it? I wonder if auld Fearchas would know what it means.'

Fearchas! Josh pounced before Niall could move, grabbing his arms and twisting them.

'Oww! Josh!'

Josh hooked Niall's legs from under his. 'Now, you talk to me! Or I'll sit on you! I want to know things.'

'Well, you only had to ask!' Niall squirmed and Josh let him go. 'That hurt!'

'All right, I'm sorry.' Josh scowled. The chase had jumbled things in his mind and he wanted to remember everything. 'For a start, what's this about the Lone Children?'

'Oh.' Niall nodded. 'It is a touch peculiar. Most island families have three or four kids. But there's Triona, Mairi, Calum and us two, all only children.'

A bit funny, Josh thought, but nothing special. Nothing weird. 'Anything else?'

'Maybe it's the families – Doinnean, Firinn, Triathan, Balachan . . . And Ros. Because you're Ailsa's family, now. But that's no mystery. Everyone on the island knows.'

Josh could have thumped him. 'What?'

'Morag hates the Five Families,' Niall said. 'We tried to stop the Falamhs getting the island. The old Celts were here first. Then the Vikings came and took island wives and island names. Then Clan MacArtair owned the place. Then the MacRaths. The last MacRath willed that the island was protected as long as birds lived here. He sold it to a millionaire who'd married a Falamh. And Morag's the last one. She's no family at all.'

'What happens when she dies?'

'No one knows. Knowing Morag, she'll try to take it with her. The Falamhs got rich by cheating the rest of us. It goes back hundreds of years, the Falamhs cheating, the Families trying to stop them.'

'Wow.' Josh swallowed. 'This is all good stuff. So, I picked the gang from the Five Families . . .'

Niall's eyes widened, innocently. 'I thought we picked ourselves?'

'Yeah, well . . . What's that smell?' Josh sniffed. 'Niall, you aren't wearing anything, are you?'

'Anything like what?'

'Like your dad's aftershave or something.'

'Josh, are you asking for the back of my fist?'

'Look, something stinks around here . . . Mairi!' Josh leapt up. 'Mairi!' He started to giggle. 'Sham-poooh!'

'Josh! Wheesht, man!'

'She must have washed everything in it! Her clothes and everything!'

'Josh!' Niall knocked him onto the grass. 'Will you shut your mouth!'

Mairi had twisted away and Niall ran after her.

'Mairi . . .' He held on to her arm. 'Come on, Mairi.'

Mairi just recognised Niall in time, her nails millimetres from his grey eyes. With only a rough brush to use on her face, she had scratched her cheeks raw. Mud spattered her feet but the rest of her gleamed spotless.

'Mairi, you look grand,' Niall said. 'Josh, doesn't she look grand?'

'I wouldn't take her to a disco.' Josh stood up. 'Not bad, I suppose.'

Without the dirt to hide it, Mairi's face blushed crimson. She twisted her skirt between her fingers.

Josh grunted. 'Come on, we're late.'

When he started to walk, Mairi slunk next to him. She watched Niall all the time and said nothing, but she really walked with them for the first time.

Calum poked his head out of the post office door. 'Dinna wait for me. I'll catch you later.' He disappeared, then snapped back, again. 'Mairi! What have you done with yourself?'

Niall smiled. 'She's a fine, bonny lass, that's what she's done with herself.'

'Man, I'd never have recognised her!'

Triona did recognise Mairi and Josh saw the big, ugly girl frown. Suddenly, Mairi was pretty and Triona did not like it. Josh sighed. It was hard work being the Boss. He would have to cheer Triona up and not upset Mairi again and help Calum to stand up to Seoras. He was not sure what he should do for Niall.

'I nearly forgot. How about a swim after school?' Josh glanced at Triona. 'OK, Tree?'

'Fine. I've swum at the Worm before. It's a grand pool.'

'Niall?'

'Swimming?' Niall's pale face looked even paler.

Josh nodded. 'You can swim, can't you?'

'Oh, sure I can! Like a fish. Underwater.'

Josh laughed but he was not sure if Niall was joking.

The first lesson was history and Calum missed it. Worrying about him, Josh almost ignored what Mrs Doinnean was saying.

'. . . for the Tilleun Sealmath. All wear your best clothes. Remember, your mams and dads will be watching . . .'

Josh stuck his hand up. 'Please, Mrs Doinnean? What's Tilleun Sealmath?'

'Has no one mentioned it, yet? You dinna know about next week . . . About St Domhnall?'

'Nope.'

'Well . . .' Mrs Doinnean looked arund the classroom. 'Who can tell Josh about St Domhnall?'

'I can.' Seoras grinned, nastily. 'He was an auld nutcase used to live in a hole on Feannag Ness. He came to turn the island Christian and got thrown off the cliff. It's a wee fairy story. The birds carried him down on their wings. Right daft, the whole thing.'

'Seoras!' Janet sighed. 'Josh, that was almost right. St Domhnall came to convert the islanders and they threw him over Feannag Ness. The birds saved his life. Every June, the birds choose a lad to be our own St Domhnall. He throws the St Domhnall doll off the cliff and asks the birds for another year's good luck.'

'What do you mean, "asks for good luck"?'

'Tilleun Sealmath.' Mairi blinked and looked surprised to hear herself talking in class.

'Go on, Mairi,' Janet nodded. 'Go on, now.'

'Gaelic . . . Bird bring good luck. They fly . . . up.'

Janet smiled. 'Good lass. You see, Josh, when the doll falls, the birds fly. The more birds, the more good luck.'

Calum arrived at school during the lunch-break, his thin face twitching at the window. He waved for the gang to join him on the wall.

'The special mail-boat came with letters for those men.' Calum grinned. 'So I waited until my dad went out and took a wee peek.'

Triona gasped. 'You never!'

'I did, too. There were three letters. I copied the names.' He handed Josh a piece of paper.

'Mr Russell King . . . and Mr Harry MacNeil.' Josh squinted at Calum's handwriting. 'Detritex International Limited. Hey, that rings a bell.'

Detritex. Josh had heard the name before but he could not remember where.

'I've got to call my dad.'

'Right now?' Triona spluttered. 'With no lunch inside us?'

'If Josh can miss his lunch, so can we.' Niall patted Calum's arm. 'That was well done, lad.'

So, twenty minutes later, Josh sat in a revolving chair in the coastguards' office, watching Calum's uncle Iain twiddling through the frequencies to find the Worm. Crackles and sputters filled the air and then Ailsa's surprised voice.

'Hello, there?'

'I'll leave you bairns to it, then.' Iain patted Josh's shoulder. 'I'll be just outside, if you need anything.' He left and closed the door behind him.

Josh pulled his hat low over his eyes. 'Yo! This is Josh the Boss, who don't give a toss, speaking to you and coming through, live on the air, everywhere!' He had a

61

really good rap rhythm going when Triona thumped him and he remembered his gran. 'Oh, hi gran. It's Josh. I've got to talk to dad.'

'You've no hurt hourself, laddie?'

'No, I'm fine. I've just got to talk to dad.'

A few minutes more and his dad's voice crackled into his ear. 'That you, Josh?'

'Dad, we know who those men are. We've got their names and who they work for . . .'

'How come?'

'Calum saw an envelope. Listen, Dad. They're called Russell King and Harry MacNeil. They both work for Detritex. I know I've heard that somewhere.'

'So have I.' Nathan thought for a minute. 'I can't remember, but it'll come to me. And Josh, I'm worried about this envelope business.'

'Calum only read the outside. He didn't open them . . .'

'And I should hope not!' Another voice snapped over the radio waves . . . Calum's dad. 'Calum! You never opened the private mail sack!'

Calum shrank behind Josh, twitching.

Josh groaned. 'Look, we had to know who they are, right? They'll never know.'

His dad sounded doubtful. 'OK, Josh. But don't do anything else like that. Is everyone coming swimming, this evening?'

'Yeah. All of us.'

'Right. And Ishbel had an idea. It's our first weekend on the island. Would you five fancy a picnic after church on Sunday? We could go to the west coast, maybe.'

Mr Balachan interrupted, eagerly. 'I'd be pleased for Calum to go with you, Mr Williams. It would do him a power of good. Myself and Mrs Balachan can visit our folks at Siarness.'

When the two men had finished talking, Josh sat back, bewildered. 'How did they do that?'

'All the radios here can hear the others,' Calum said. 'Now, let's get back. I dinna care to be late twice in the one day.'

As soon as the final bell rang, Josh and the gang set off for the Worm, collecting swimsuits as they went. The sky swirled dark grey and gusts of wind surged up from the ground, dragging at Josh's legs. Like walking through water.

'It's going to be a fine storm,' Triona said. 'Can you no feel it, Josh?'

'I don't suppose we'll hear it, in the cellar.' Josh wondered why she was grinning. 'What?'

'You'd hear an island storm if you burrowed under the rocks like a wee rabbit.'

She was right. The gang had hardly changed into swimming gear when thunder rocked the Worm on its foundations. The ground shivered and the cellar light blinked. For a moment, the five friends stood still.

'Wow! That was loud.'

Triona balanced on the pool edge. 'We might be down here in the dark. That's what the candles are for.'

The swimming-pool lurked at the back of the cellar, below the big reception room. A bit spooky, really. If this had been London, Josh would have turned his nose up at the square hole in the concrete. But it was his own pool and that made a difference. He decided to play safe and scuttled around the room, lighting candles.

'We've only had electricity since '85. Before that, it was all bottled gas and peat.'

Triona pretended not to care if anyone saw her dive

but, as soon as Josh looked towards her, she threw herself into the pool. She shattered the water like an elephant seal.

'Come in! This is grand!'

Calum did not have to be asked twice. Whooping, skinny legs folded to his chest, he dive-bombed the pool over Triona's head. To Josh's amazement, he swam tadpole fast.

'Josh, come on in!' Calum threw water at him. 'It's real fine!'

'I'm coming.' Josh winced at another rattle of thunder. The lights flickered. 'You OK, Niall?'

Niall had undressed and pulled on swimming trunks faster than anyone, as if he had to move that fast or not move at all. Now he sat at the shallow end, pale head resting on his knees. Arms wrapped around his shins. Mairi stood behind him, too worried about him to be shy. Josh padded to her side and Niall's head came up, turning to face them.

Josh tried a smile of encouragement. 'Niall, Mairi and I'll get in first.'

Niall just looked at him. A ghost, Josh thought, all silvery hair, grey eyes, white face.

'Come on, Mairi. You go on his left.'

Mairi slid over the edge, her super-scrubbed plaits floating behind her.

'We'll grab a hand each.' Josh stepped into the water and yelped. 'It's freezing! I thought you said it was grand!'

'You're soft, that's all.' Triona swam past, kicking her big feet. 'It's fine and warm.'

Josh shuddered and the lights went out. 'Oh great!'

Calum paddled across the deep end, grinning. Candlelight sharpened his face. He looked like a swimming pixie. 'Man, this feels fine!'

Niall's eyes clenched shut and his arms stretched forwards. Josh and Mairi gripped a cold hand each and pulled. Without a sound, Niall slid over the edge.

'I'll teach you to swim, Niall,' Josh said. 'Then you won't be scared.'

'I told you, I can swim.' Niall's eyes stayed closed. 'Underwater. I'm real fine at going underwater.'

Mairi felt it first. Then Niall's grey eyes flew open. And Josh swept through the sky, peering down through a bird's eyes. He knew what sort of bird this time, but then he forgot. Flying made him forget.

Water glinted below him – Niall's loch, Loch Sgailinne. The Triathan house stood on the shore next to a crooked pier with a boat tied to it.

'Careful! Not safe!' The bird's frightened squeal rang in Josh's head. 'Boy fall!'

What boy? Josh squinted and saw the little boy standing on the pier edge. A tall, blond man jumped into the boat, rowing angrily away. Josh gasped. That was a young Dr Hector! So, the pale-haired boy was Niall.

'Six years old,' Niall said.

'Not safe!' The bird squealed louder. 'Not safe! Boy fall!'

Josh's heart thudded. He watched little Niall sigh and turn away. And then the pier shivered. Niall screamed, 'Dad! Dad!' as it tilted sideways.

'Hey!' Josh tried to yell. 'Hey! Dr Hector!'

Dr Hector stopped rowing. Too late. The pier collapsed and Niall crashed into the water.

'It was cold, Josh.' Niall, far away. 'There was ice in the loch, that morning.'

Little Niall clung to the breaking wood until a plank slapped him down. Then no pier, no Niall, and the bird squealed away.

Water flashed past, then grass, tree-tops, sky. The bird turned, steeply, as Dr Hector dived, swimming frantically for the pier.

On the other side of the lake, a dark shape hid in the brambles . . . Mairi. She watched Dr Hector dive again and again, finally cough and choke to the surface with his son in his arms. Dead son. The pale-haired little boy did not breathe.

Hector's yells brought Fiona running, her red hair terribly bright against her son's white face. The two doctors attacked Niall like muggers, thumping him over their knees. Eyes wide, Mairi crept forward until she stood beside the little boy's body. It seemed like years before Niall squirmed and coughed, sobbing back to life.

The candle-light brightened and Josh heard Calum hoot with laughter, Triona splash after him. Mairi watched Josh's face, silently.

'So now you know.' Niall rested his hands, trembling, on the pool edge. 'I nearly died, Josh.'

'I saw,' Josh said. 'And Mairi was there when it happened.'

'I never knew.' Niall tried to give Mairi a smile but his lips would not move. 'I remember going under the last time. The plank nearly knocked me out but not quite. I could still feel when I breathed water. It burned something cruel. And I drowned. And it's going to happen again, Josh. I'll be on my own, again. And this time, no one will save me.'

A week ago, if someone had said that to Josh, he would have told them not to be so stupid. But he had seen – *seen* with that bird's eyes – little Niall drowning.

Candles flickered around the white-washed walls, dragging crazy shadows from table legs and old chairs. One shadow spread, a darker velvet shape sliding over the concrete. A cat's paw. Niall gasped as it fell over him, so cold that Josh felt it on his own, wet shoulders. The claws curled for Niall's left eye and Josh yelled . . . 'No!'

Scars. He saw four scars slash into Niall's face, where the cat clawed him. Josh shut his eyes tight. When he opened them, the scars had gone.

'Are you all right, over there?' Calum swam towards them. 'Come and swim!'

Anger came from nowhere, clenching Josh's fists. Cat's claws! Drowning! 'Niall!' Josh had had enough. 'Don't you say that! I won't let it happen again! And I'm the Boss, Niall.'

Niall shivered but his smile worked, this time. 'All right, Boss.'

'I mean it, Niall! I'm not having you drowning on me.'

'Josh, I promise I won't drown if I can possibly avoid it.'

Josh opened his mouth, then spluttered as Triona ducked him. He remembered that he had the others to think about and swam after Calum and pinched Mairi's toes. Niall joined in and laughed and messed about but only in the shallow end. He did not go out of his depth and Josh did not blame him.

The lights flickered on a few minutes later and Josh's dad appeared, wearing yellow oilskins. Like a fisherman, Josh thought.

'In case you kids haven't noticed, there's a gale out there. Triona, your dad's here to take you and Calum home. I'll drive Niall back myself.' He gave Mairi his wobbly grin. 'Mairi, you'd better stay the night with us. Will your grandfather be worried?'

Mairi shook her head. 'He know . . . I safe.'

*

67

The sky over the island simmered browny-black, striped with white ripples of lightning. In the kitchen, Father Kevin drank a quick mug of tea. He suddenly looked a lot like Triona, all bony strength, woolly hair, big, blotchy face.

'Come on, lassie.' He helped Triona into a sou'wester and oilskin coat. 'And you, Calum. There's a grand wee breeze blowing. Did you enjoy your swim, now?'

Triona nodded. 'It's been fine. And we'll see you tomorrow, Josh. At the ceilidh.'

Josh glanced at Ishbel. 'That's that party thing, isn't it?'

'We hold one every Saturday, Josh. But tomorrow is for you and your dad.' She patted his damp hair. 'Now, say good-night to your friends. Mairi can help Mam with the dinner.'

Few people struggled to the Worm that evening. Nathan returned from Niall's house making pirate noises – 'Avast there me hearties! Ah-ha!' Water streamed from his oilskins and his hair was pearled all over with raindrops.

Josh wondered what he was going to do with Mairi for the rest of the evening. After he had shown her around upstairs, he let Ailsa take over. Mairi peeled potatoes and carried plates to the big kitchen table. She did not say a word, just nodded or shook her head when Ishbel offered her more stew and scones. Every time Nathan smiled at her, she blushed and hid her face between her shoulders. Then Josh had an idea.

'You can see Niall's place from upstairs. Want a look?'

Mairi nodded and her eyes shone.

'Come on, then.'

The storm flew on tearing gusts of wind, throwing bucketfuls of rain into the windows. Every few minutes, the lights flickered wildly. The Worm's emergency generator only supplied the public rooms, so Josh stuffed his dad's torch into his pocket, just in case, and led Mairi back up to the guest room.

'It's best at night. You can see the lights.' Josh knelt on the windowsill. 'Look, just over the hill. You can see the roof and the top windows.'

Mairi slid next to him, pressing her face against the glass.

'Can you see it?'

'Yes.' And she smiled.

Josh gulped. He had never seen Mairi smile. She looked quite good. Pretty, like a wild fox might be pretty. Mairi always looked dangerous.

'You really like Niall, don't you? I mean, I suppose everyone likes him, he's a good kid. But you like him more than anyone else does.'

She looked pleased and the smile stretched a bit wider. 'Grandad said . . . Triathan first boy jump . . . from Feannag Ness.'

'Jump?' Josh frowned. 'St Domhnall got thrown over.'

'Before,' Mairi said. 'Long time before.' She leaned forwards and heaved the sash window open.

The gale screamed in, stinging Josh's eyes and soaking his shirt. Too startled to say anything, he watched Mairi stretch both arms into the rain, as if she wanted to reach through the storm, up the hill and into Niall's home.

'Mairi! You'll freeze!'

She nodded and helped him drag the window back down. The room was quiet suddenly, and Josh bit his lip.

'You heard what Niall said, about drowning again?'

The smile melted from her face and she nodded.

'And Seoras is going to flatten him, one of these days.'

'If . . . if he hurt Niall . . .' Her hands twisted on the sill. 'I kill him.'

6   Ceilidh

Josh woke up on Saturday morning, smiling before he opened his eyes. Spog pecked at the window with her sharp, little beak but he was ready for her. He crumbled a chunk of bread onto the window-sill.

'There you go, greedy-guts.' Spog gobbled happily. 'Nice bird. Who's a pretty bird, then?' Josh touched her warm wing, stroking down the long, flight feathers with his thumb. And yelled. 'Ow! Ow! That's blood!'

'Josh?' Ishbel peered around the bedroom door. 'Ach, dear! Has she hurt you?'

'Only bitten a lump out of my thumb!' He stuck his poor thumb under Ishbel's nose. 'And I'd just fed her, as well.'

Ishbel smiled at the fluttering gull. 'Well, she'd be grateful for the food, pet, but she's no tame budgie. Mairi's gone home, by the way. Did you show her Niall's house, last night?'

'Yeah.' Josh frowned. 'It's the first time she's smiled.'

'Niall's a nice boy,' Ishbel said. 'But I can feel the fear in him. You know he near drowned?'

Josh nodded. 'Mairi was there.'

'I never knew that.' Ishbel's brows rose. 'Maybe that's why she's so protective of him. Seeing him brought back from death like that.'

'She said if anyone hurt Niall, she'd kill them.' He glanced at Ishbel's face. 'And she really meant it.'

70

'Aye, she would.' Ishbel patted his shoulder. 'Now, we've a fine load of work to do. There's cleaning and tidying and cooking and shopping. It's a grand way of working up an appetite.'

Ishbel was right about his appetite. By the time Josh had helped his dad and Willy-John to clean the public rooms and finished his homework, he could have eaten Liath's pony-nuts. He had dressed for work in his white sweatshirt with 'Yo!' printed on the front, baggy trousers and black lace-up boots. Serious style.

'Will you cycle into Roncamas for me, Josh? There's some things I only use fresh.' Ailsa pulled a bag from her apron. 'This will keep you going. Pan drops and soor ploom and half a bannock with butter.'

'I could do with some fresh air.' Josh tossed the bag between his fingers. 'I'll eat it watching the boats.'

Outside, he gave his bike a quick safety check. Squatting next to the back wheel, he felt eyes . . . The big crow stared at him, less than a metre away. In the shadow of the pub, it looked a bit tatty, frayed around the edges. When Josh reached towards it, it squawked and shuffled backwards and he felt its voice in his head. 'I'm no your bird!' Before he could tell himself he was crazy, it had vanished.

Josh peddled over the cobbles and into slurping mud. What he needed was a good fast ride to take vanishing crows out of his head. A bicycle-bell rang behind him.

'Do you need a hand at all, Josh?' Niall free-wheeled onto the bridge.

Josh scanned Niall's bike from handlebars to tail-light. 'Nice wheels. Looks fast.'

'Is it a race you're after? In all this muck?' Niall groaned. 'I suppose we'd have a fine, soft landing if we fell. All right, I'll race you back and welcome.'

'You're on!' Josh steered to Niall's left. 'And what're pan drops and soor ploom? And what's a bannock?'

'A pan drop's a white mint, soor ploom are bitter-sweet candies and a bannock's a round loaf.' Niall tried not to look hungry. 'You might want to share?'

'You'll have to work for it.'

Niall sighed. 'I always do.'

Niall helped Josh load the two bike-bags with eggs, milk, butter and other bits and bobs for the ceilidh, then they walked to the pier and sat on the sea-wall, munching soor ploom. The fishermen had stretched their nets over the wall to dry. Several men sat repairing tears with long needles, the older men smoking pipes, the younger ones cigarettes. Josh decided that the Worm should be No Smoking. It was time someone told the islanders about lung cancer. A powerful smell of fish, salt-water and engine oil washed in with the waves and he inhaled it, greedily.

'If you come here at dusk or dawn, you might see the otters. Their wee, whiskery faces pop up around the pier, there.' Niall nodded past the ferry moorings. 'They like swimming around piers. They're at your place as well.'

'Under our pier?'

'Aye, they're a grand sight.' Niall watched Josh's face. 'Are you liking life here, Josh? I suppose it's a big change from London? You're no homesick for the bright lights?'

Josh swallowed a lump of mint. 'Bright lights? Nah, you can keep them. This place is OK. I haven't been bored, anyway.'

'That's true.' Niall laughed. 'It's been fair interesting, this last week. Now let's be off before the butter melts.'

They behaved themselves until they had passed the post

office, the last building on the road, then they stood on their pedals and spun forwards, wheels slithering.

'First one to the bridge,' Niall yelled.

Josh has been the fastest biker in his class. After seeing Niall so shaken in the swimming-pool, he had decided the thinner boy was no competition. Wrong. Niall had natural skill.

'Hey!' Josh pumped the pedals, furiously. 'Hoi! That's not fair!'

Niall breezed away from him, raised one hand and waved his fingertips. Yellow mud splattered Josh's front wheel, over his fingers, up his arms and all the way to his hat. His specs sprouted yellow measles.

'That's not fair!' Josh spat mud. 'Yug!'

It all happened so fast. Josh lifted a hand to wipe his specs and Spog dive-bombed him, squealing. It meant something was wrong.

'Hey, Niall!'

Too late. Niall vanished around the bend in the road. And yelled, 'Josh, stop!'

Josh braked, hard. Skidding, fighting to stay in control, he heard the horrible metal-and-slush slither as Niall's bike hit the road. Spog dived again as Josh swung around the corner, expecting . . . Not expecting Niall to be sitting on the road, at Morag Falamh's feet, his head centimetres from the hard wooden bridge-post. Niall's bike lay in a twisted heap, thick with mud and torn grass.

'Are you bairns playing, then?' Morag said. 'Now isn't that grand?'

'I could have hit her . . . She never moved.' Blood speckled Niall's knuckles. 'Half the road's in my hand.'

Josh jumped off his bike. 'Are you all right, mate?'

'Fine. Just all muck and gore.' Niall stood up, breathing hard. 'I nearly hit the bridge!'

Morag smiled. 'Ach, so you did. You could have cracked your skull and slid down into the burn, into all that water.' She watched Niall's face turn grey with horror and laughed. 'That would have been a sore shame!'

Josh's skin crawled. 'You did it on purpose! You knew we were coming and you stood there on purpose!'

'Prove it.' Spit spattered her lips. 'And this is my land! I'll stand where I please! And here's a wee word of warning. Dinna get in my way!' Spog spun past her and she lashed out, a vicious swipe that clipped the little gull's wing. 'You'll know what I mean tomorrow. And no wee birdies will help you then.'

Morag sauntered over the bridge. At the other side, she slid onto the passenger seat of the big car and sped back to Loch Falamh.

Spog landed on Josh's shoulder.

'Spog tried to tell us, Niall. If we hadn't been going so fast . . .'

'Aye, it's no her fault. She's a grand wee bird.' Niall dragged his bike out of the mud. 'Ach, look at this! I hope the eggs are with you, Josh. Or there'll be a grand omelette in my bag.'

'Your hands are a real mess.'

Niall grimaced. 'There's so much hate in that woman. You know, Josh, Falamh's the Gaelic for "empty". The Falamhs have always been squeezed dry of anything good. My mam says Morag can't have bairns and that's another reason she hates us. I canna help feeling sorry for her. I've never seen her happy.'

'Happy?' Josh shook his head. 'I hope she's sick as a parrot!'

As Josh had expected, Ailsa took one look at Niall and dragged him towards the hall.

'Poor, wee soul! You're that peelie-wally, you'd pass for a ghost! Josh, go and tell his mam where he is and bring some dry clothes back.' She gave Niall a mighty hug. 'Dinna fret yourself, laddie. I'll take care of you.'

Josh grinned at the look on Niall's face. 'Don't worry, Niall. You can stay and help with the ceilidh.'

Niall came back into the kitchen half an hour later, his knuckles yellow where Ailsa had dabbed them with iodine. With his hair spiky-damp, his shirt and tie, he looked a bit like David Bowie. Niall could really wear clothes. But Josh looked better in hats. Niall had tried the black leather on the day before and fallen about laughing. You had to be serious to wear a good hat.

'You OK, Niall?'

'Fine.'

'You'd say that if you'd broken your neck.' Josh frowned at him. 'I mean, honestly. Are you OK?'

'A wee bit shoogly-legged.' He lowered his voice. 'One thing, Josh. What Morag said, about tomorrow. It sounded like a threat.'

'She was trying to scare us, that's all.'

'Well, she made a grand job of it.'

'Yeah, I know what you mean.' Josh twiddled his specs, thinking about Morag Falamh. 'But she can't do anything, can she? I mean, she can't go around sticking crow's heads on everyone's doors. Tell you what, let's forget her for tonight. There's loads to do.'

With Niall to help him, Josh enjoyed getting ready for the ceilidh. He wondered how far he could push Niall before the other boy noticed. Pretty far. Niall just could not say no.

'Give us a hand with this, Niall? Niall, can you reach that box? Can you shift those trays? You've missed a bit . . .'

His dad pulled warning faces but Josh ignored him.

'Hey, Niall. You know what really needs doing?'

The four 'menfolk' had just moved the piano across the stage. Willy-John and Nathan sat on the stage-edge, getting their breaths back and talking about spotlights.

'What?'

'Well . . .' Josh sat on the piano stool. 'It would look really good if you went outside . . .'

'Oh aye?'

'With a brush . . .'

'Fine, so far.'

Josh grinned. 'And cleaned all the seals' flippers.'

'Josh!' Nathan groaned. 'That isn't even funny!'

Niall's face changed from eager-to-help to disbelief to a wicked grin. 'Right!' He lunged and grabbed Josh under the arms.

'Arghh! No . . . Stop it!' Josh rolled around, clinging to the stool for dear life. 'Ow-howw! Dad, help!'

But his dad just sat back, giggling, as Niall tickled Josh's ribs.

People arrived for the ceilidh shortly after. Father Kevin, Janet and Triona came first, with a large bottle of something.

'Nathan, you and me and Hector might sup on this, later.' Father Kevin patted the dark glass. 'Something a wee bit special you mainlanders don't get a sight of.'

Nathan grinned. 'I'm all for something a bit special.'

Josh was soon too busy welcoming kids from school to think about anything else. Apart from Mairi, all the gang were there and they helped out, carrying trays of goodies to the people in the back room. Up on the stage, Willy-John arranged himself around an old accordion. His fingers spidered over the keys and a happy tumble of notes filled the room. A man with a drum sat on the piano stool and joined in. Soon, people's feet were tapping.

'That's not bad.' Josh filled Calum's tray. 'I could dance to that.'

'Just you wait. My dad's outside, tuning his fiddle.'

'Your dad?'

But Calum had already slid through a gap in the crowd. Josh gazed around the big reception room. Women nursed babies on their laps, old men smoked pipes, kids danced as if they were at a disco. In fact, they danced harder than kids at a disco, really throwing themselves about and yelling. Josh quite fancied himself as a dancer. He wondered if Ishbel would show him the steps.

It was a night for surprises. Triona had squeezed into a lace-collared dress, the first time Josh had seen her in anything pretty. It looked awful and she knew it.

Triona shrugged. 'My mam likes it. I dinna mind, but I'm happier in jeans.'

Seoras arrived with two older brothers and about twenty cousins. At first, he ignored Josh and went to take a good look at his dad.

'Does your dad play anything, then? Or sing?'

Josh shook his head. 'He's terrible. I mean, his voice is evil! He can't even dance.'

'Well, that's something.'

Josh realised that Seoras was pleased. 'Have a peanut, Seoras.'

'I dinna mind if I do.' Seoras dug a fistful of nuts out of the dish. 'This is no so bad, after all.' He turned and slouched into the party.

'Ach, now you'll see something.' Ailsa wrapped her arm around Josh's shoulder. 'There's Archie and Peigi Balachan.'

'What? Old . . .?' Josh stopped himself. 'I mean, they're so . . . stiff . . . And they're both deaf.'

'You'll be surprised, Josh. And dinna be so quick to judge. Prejudice blinds folk to the richness of life. My old dad told me that. You miss a lot if you sneer at folk different from yourself.'

'Sorry.' Josh frowned. 'I hadn't thought of it like that.'

Archie Balachan walked onto the stage, gave Willy-John a shy little smile, then propped his fiddle under his chin. Slowly, his head started to nod, finding a beat, and the drummer took it up, then Willy-John. Archie's foot stamped and his bow swooped into a wild jig. Just below the stage, his wife curtseyed and started to dance.

Josh's jaw dropped. 'Hey!'

Calum appeared at his side, freckled face glowing. 'Josh. What do you think?'

'They're magic!' Josh grinned. 'Wow! Look at your mum move!'

Peigi danced on her toes, pointing them, crossing them, hopping in an invisible square over the wooden floor . . . Like tap-dancing on tiptoe, Josh thought. Everyone clapped in time and he felt his own hands join in. Men stood to stamp and whoop. When the tune ended, you could have heard the cheers in London.

An hour later, out of breath after Triona had dragged him through a Highland Reel, Josh realised that his dad had vanished. He found Ishbel chatting with Fiona and Janet.

'Ishbel, where's Dad?'

'I think the men are supping that auld bottle. Let's go and see.'

Josh followed the women into the quieter air of the front rooms. They heard giggling and Ishbel sighed.

'Ach, I thought so! They're seeing how much Nathan can take before he falls over.'

Ailsa had found the men a few minutes before and stood, hands on hips, glaring down at them. Father Kevin's woolly hair stood in tufts, his face red and shiny, like a wet tomato. Next to him, Dr Hector's handsome, blond head wore the silliest grin Josh had ever seen . . . until he looked at his dad's big, soppy smile.

Ailsa groaned. 'Will you look at them! Grown men! Fou as puggies, the three of them!'

Josh hooted with laughter. 'Dad! You should see your face!'

His dad tried to look serious. 'Hi there, Jossss . . .' His tongue had trouble saying Josh. 'Hello, Jossssh.'

Ishbel sighed. 'You'll have a fine head on you tomorrow, my lad. What a waste of a fine evening! You'll not one of you remember a minute of it.'

Nathan's face changed. He blinked a few times and rubbed his nose. 'That's it, Josssh. Waste.'

'Dad, what are you on about?'

'Jossh, listen.' His dad scowled. 'Detritex Inter . . . Inter . . . Those men.'

'Yeah?'

'Waste.' Nathan spoke very carefully. 'Detritex is into waste . . . Atomic, chemical . . . Nasty stuff, Josssh.'

Ailsa moved away from the table. 'I'm calling the Council in here, right now. You men sober up!'

Fiona shook her head, horrified. 'Ach, my good Lord! If they're thinking of dumping their waste here! I canna bear to think on it!'

Josh stiffened. He had already see what the Detritex men wanted to do to the island. The tolleun had shown him a vision of concrete bunkers full of poison and a dead sea. For once, Josh could think of nothing to say.

A couple of mugs of coffee later, the three men seemed almost sensible. At least Josh's dad could say 'Josh' without knotting his tongue. The rest of the Council sat with them – Calum's uncle Iain, Tomas Hegarty and Elly Nelly Clagan.

'So, these men are waste dumpers,' Iain Balachan said. 'And if they're staying with Morag Falamh . . .'

'But they canna do it!' Elly Nelly shook her head. 'So long as there's birds here, we're protected. Isn't that so, Janet?'

'It's right enough. And Morag knows it. I canna understand it at all.'

'Well, one thing's . . .' Father Kevin waved his hand and knocked his glass over. 'Ooops . . . One thing's for certain. They must think there's a way around it. Or they'd no waste time and money staying here. So, what do we do?'

Ailsa had hoisted herself onto the bar. She sat there, feet swinging. 'We keep our eyes open. The birds will stay so long as we call them over Feannag Ness. That happens this Thursday. And I'm starting to wonder if that's why Morag came back, just now. So, until then, we keep our eyes open.'

The ceilidh ended at midnight but the Doinneans, Balachans and Triathans stayed for another hour, helping to clear the mess. Josh reminded everyone about the picnic after church, then staggered to bed, his mind full of Detritex, poison cats, Niall's bike covered in mud and Morag Falamh's mad, cruel eyes.

7   Silver Beak

Josh enjoyed church. The building was nothing like his old church, in London. For a start it had been built eight hundred years ago. It was very plain, very white, with a slab of stone for the altar. Father Kevin preached a good sermon, about the world being a living body and people being its heart. If people poisoned the body, the heart would die. All good stuff. And Father Kevin got excited about it, waving his fist and knocking his hymn-book onto the floor. People bumped heads to pick it up. Josh guessed that happened a lot. He liked Father Kevin.

Mairi was already waiting at the Worm, patting the ponies over the stable doors. Josh was sorry she had not come to the ceilidh and decided to invite her to the next one. The gang should stick together. Mairi helped Ishbel to harness Liath and Dubh to the big cart and Ailsa to load it with food for the picnic. Then she picked up everything Nathan dropped, following him three times around the cart as he juggled bags of peanuts with Calum.

'What's got ten legs, purple spots and eats rock?' Calum asked. 'A ten-legged, purple-spotted rock eater!'

Josh screamed and thumped him.

'Josh!' Ishbel pulled him away, laughing. 'Josh, your dad and I were thinking. If you all like, we could go to Beinn Dubh? You can wish on the thorn tree.'

'It's good luck, right?'

Calum threw a bag of peanuts at him. Missed. Mairi picked it up.

'Now you all have a grand time.' Ailsa gave Josh a bone-creaking hug. 'If I wasn't so busy, I'd come with you. Take care, mind.'

Nathan grinned. 'Don't worry, Ailsa, I'm too silly for anything dangerous.'

Josh snorted. 'Too right!'

Ishbel took the ponies above Niall's house and onto the cat-chase road. Today, real sunlight glittered over Loch Sgailinne and Loch Darach shone silver around its fairy island. The cart was followed, again, but this time by a pair of birds – one big, one small and nippy – the two home gulls. Ishbel steered the cart off the road at the foot of Beinn Dubh.

'It doesn't look all that high.' Josh pointed his specs up the sloping grass. 'I can see the thorn tree.'

'Beinn Dubh is the gentlest hill on the island. And full of rabbits, so mind your ankles.' Ishbel spread the table-cloth on the grass. 'After we've eaten, there's good luck ribbons for you to fasten on the thorns. Now, come and eat, hungry ones.'

She might have meant the gang, but Josh knew better. Flapping and squawking, Spog and Goath dropped onto the turf, gobbling Ishbel's gift of bread and sardines.

'Typical!' Josh shook his head. 'Typical! The birds eat before the rest of us.'

Everyone laughed and he pulled a face. There was no point arguing, anyway. The whole island was crazy about birds.

After lunch, Triona and Calum led the way up Beinn Dubh. Ishbel had given them red ribbons, knotted with pieces of lucky paper and feathers, to tie on the thorn bush. On the lower slopes, black marbles of rabbit-droppings hinted at burrows. Mairi pointed and Josh laughed at a sudden, white bob-tail racing away from him. Then the slope steepened.

''S'not . . . as low . . . as I thought.' Josh puffed and panted, on hands and knees over a mound of rock. 'Tree! Slow down!'

Triona's heavy feet clomped even faster. 'You're no so fit, are you?'

'You don't get mountains . . . in London. I'm knackered.' He sat down, wiping his face on his sleeve. 'How much further?'

'Come on.' Niall hauled Josh upright. 'We'll sit down at the top. There's a grand view over the island.'

Too breathless to grumble, Josh staggered after him. The sharp grass cut his fingers and hidden rocks skidded from under his feet. Once, he stood too tall and Mairi thumped him in the ribs to stop him from falling. She grinned at him and danced ahead like a mountain goat.

'The top . . . Great.' Josh fell full-length, letting the sun lick his face. 'My legs . . . like jelly . . . Can't move.'

'Get your breath back, man. Dinna waste it blethering.' Calum sat next to him. 'And look at that view!'

At the foot of the hill, trees led into Loch Darach and to hundreds of small sequins of water, tiny lakes that turned into marsh, then sandy scrub, then the sea. Long white-sand beaches stretched down the west coast, into the Atlantic.

'It's a fine breeding ground for birds, the west coast.' Triona pointed over Josh's shoulder. 'Those patches like snow. All birds.'

'I didn't know the island in Loch Darach was that big . . . And trees on it.'

'Eilean Sithiche,' Mairi said. 'No one goes there.'

Josh was surprised. 'You know, Mairi, you're getting better at talking. Ishbel says the island's unlucky.'

Calum nodded. 'Mairi's right, no one goes there. For one thing, Loch Darach's full of deep currents. The water's that black, if you put your arm in, you canna see your fingers on the end of it. And cold! Man, I'd no swim in Darach if you paid me!'

'People have died,' Triona said. 'Some teenagers took a boat out, for a dare. Two drowned. That was when Alex Ros built the swimming-pool under the Worm, so folk could learn to swim safely.'

'He sounds like a good bloke.' Josh felt better. He stretched his legs. 'Hey, I can see Loch Falamh . . . And Morag's place.'

To the north of Loch Darach, a burn led to the dead Loch Falamh. Morag's big house, Falamh Taigh, sat on the eastern shore, two storeys high with three square chimneys.

'We'd better move. Tie your ribbon to a branch, Josh, and make a wish.'

'Oh yeah?'

But Josh followed Triona to the scraggy thorn bush. Hundreds of ribbons whipped among its branches, some with paper and feathers, some knotted with white stones, all of them red – the lucky colour. They blurred into red mist and sang, whining and howling in the wind. Josh listened. The clatter and flap of ribbons sounded like birds flying. Wings beating. A hundred pairs of wings. He winced and it was just a thorn tree, again, old ribbon in its branches.

Mairi loosened a plait and tugged a black hair free. She tied it to the highest branch she could reach, screwed her eyes shut and made a wish. Her lips moved and one of the words was 'Niall'. When Josh glanced to his left, Niall pretended not to have noticed.

Careful of the thorns, Josh tied his own ribbon to a branch. 'Hey, look! The eagles!' He forgot to wish for anything, trotting back along the hill top.

Triona had already moved to the west side of the summit. She yelped and pointed. 'I can see Morag! Near the tolleun at the top of Darach.'

Everyone hurried to join her, peering over the water to the tiny figure of Morag Falamh.

'She's on her knees,' Josh said. 'What's she doing on her knees? Praying?'

'She's up to no good, that's what she's doing,' Calum shuddered. 'I dinna mind saying it, that auld witch scares me daft.'

The eagles circled high over Beinn Dubh, then swerved west, into the wide, blue sky.

'They'll fly right over her.' Josh looked back at the thorn bush. 'Do you really get your wish, from that thing?'

'That's what folk say.' Niall frowned at him. 'Why?'

'Well, then. I wish we could look through the eagles' eyes and see what she's doing.'

He had not expected it to work and never that quickly. But they were all there, up in the eagles' eyes, watching Morag Falamh. And hearing her. The eagles would not know what she was saying, but the five goggling friends on Beinn Dubh understood every word.

Morag had burned a circle into the grass, the singed earth concentrating her power. At each of the compass points sat a different magic charm – a rock at north, a lighted candle at south, a dish of salt water to the east and a dried sprig of mistletoe to the west. Morag crouched in the middle, beside the neglected tolleun, rattling something between her palms.

'Cat's bones, cat's bones, who will it be? Who will the birds choose? Now let me see . . .'

She opened her fingers and scattered broken bones onto the ground. Before she could see what the bones told her, eagle-shadows swept over her hands. She leapt up, furious, and the eagles spun away.

'Shoot!' Josh shook his head. 'That's it. I didn't think it would work.'

'There's a powerful lot of magic around, right now.' Triona rubbed her arms with her fists. 'You know what she's up to? Trying to see who the birds will pick for St Domhnall, tomorrow morning. I'll tell you, Josh, the way you've been gathering magic, it might be you.'

'Me!' Josh jumped backwards. 'No chance! I'm not getting mixed up with anything else weird.'

'You just made a wish come true, Josh.' Niall smiled at him. 'You dinna think that's a wee bit weird?'

'You shut up!' Josh stomped away. 'I don't mind making things happen, myself. But I'm not getting picked for something like that by a dirty old bird. And that's final . . . Hey!'

'What?' Niall walked after him. 'Hey what?'

'What's wrong with those two? Goath and Spog are going crazy.'

'Josh! Josh!' Mairi knocked him flying, screaming into Gaelic.

'Ach no! Look at that!' Niall slid to his knees. 'Josh, look back at Roncamas. What size of fire would throw that much smoke in the air?'

A huge fire, Josh thought. A really, really horrible huge fire. Black snarls of smoke coiled upwards, so wrong against the blue sky that he felt ill. He sat there and did not know what to say. It looked like a disaster movie. The smoke looked alive, a curling mass of dark muscle pushing into the air.

Triona scowled. 'It's on the east of town, near the harbour . . . I think it's the post office.'

Calum's face turned perfectly white. He looked from Josh to Niall to Triona, then at a suddenly quiet Mairi. Without a word, he swivelled and fled for the edge of the hill.

'Be careful! Calum, don't run!'

'It's no good, Josh. He's too scared to listen. And if it is the post office . . .' Triona shook her head. 'It's a grand, dark cloud of smoke.'

'Isn't there a fire brigade in this place?'

'Just a wee engine near the lifeboat. They'll pump sea-water out of the harbour.' Triona watched Niall and Mairi sprint down the hill. 'We'd better go. Your mam and dad will want to drive back and help.'

Josh nodded and, for one second, frowned back towards Morag Falamh. If she was here, she could not have set fire to anything in Roncamas. Something bothered him but it had slid out of his head before he could think about it. He gritted his teeth and set off down Beinn Dubh in a skidding, hopping, slither and run.

By the time Ishbel drove into Roncamas, the worst was over. Most of the town had turned out to help, but now people stood around, muttering to each other. Nathan hurried forwards to see if he could do anything.

Dr Hector, blond head black with soot, stood on the road. 'I tell you, Nathan, that was no usual fire. It melted the radio to a puddle. I've never felt such heat.'

Ailsa hugged Calum to her chest, bits of ash floating

from her hair. 'It's all right, lad, your mam and dad are safe. Willy-John's taken them to the Worm.'

Calum blinked back the tears. 'All my things! All my joke books . . . my cartoons and everything.' He gazed at Josh helplessly. 'All gone!'

Mairi slid forwards and stroken Calum's hand. 'You . . . safe. Only things gone . . .'

The post office had burned to the ground. Shaking their heads, the first islanders moved away from the smoking pile of rubble. A few wooden beams still cracked open, glinting red under the black. Iain Balachan's men hosed them down, clouds of steam hissing over the road. The taste and stink of smoke swirled into throats and noses. Josh coughed and blinked.

'Do you think it was deliberate, Hector?' Nathan asked. 'I know I've not been here very long . . . But maybe we should get the authorities in on this?'

'I canna think about it, just now . . . Kevin and Fiona have gone with the Balachans. Janet is asking folk to help with clothes and such. I just canna believe this could happen here!' Hector rubbed his eyes. 'I've a load of smoke in me. I should check myself out, and all the others . . .'

Ishbel wiped her own eyes. 'Poor Calum! And Archie and Peigi! They lived for that place.'

'Aye, that they did.' Hector managed a smile. 'And they're in the best hands anyone could hope for, with Kevin and Fiona and Ailsa. No, we canna do anything unless the Council agrees. And this week we'll no want nosy policemen underfoot. Tomorrow's the choosing of our St Domhnall.'

Niall touched his dad's arm. 'Dad, are you all right? Your eyes are that red . . .'

'I'm fine, Niall. What a filthy, filthy thing to happen to such nice folk!'

'We canna let it spoil things.' Ishbel's chin came up. 'Archie and Peigi would agree with that. We need a good holy week. We'll thank the birds and have good luck next year. After Thursday, the Council can decide what to do.'

Hector nodded. 'I think that's for the best. Now, you bairns go and look after Calum. He'll want a lot of comforting.'

'Yeah . . .' Josh felt the others move closer to him – Triona and Mairi and Niall, all standing together. 'And Calum's in our gang! No one does this to someone in the gang!' He turned, fast, and ran after Granny Ailsa.

'And I'm the Boss,' Josh thought. 'I shouldn't have let this happen. I've got to do something about it.'

Josh yawned his way downstairs on Monday morning to find a procession in the hall. People carried bundles of clothes, shoes, even shaving-tackle and hairbrushes.

'What's happening?' Josh squeezed along the wall to Mrs Balachan. 'What's all this?'

She shook her head. 'All these folk bringing us things! I never knew we had so many friends.'

Over breakfast, Josh learned that the Balachans would live at Iain's place until a new post office was built. Unfortunately, Iain had only one room to spare. To Calum's delight, Ishbel had invited him to stay at the Worm.

'We'll build on the auld site.' Archie tucked into hot, salty porridge. 'It'll cost a bonny penny but we were well insured.'

Peigi sighed. 'I never knew we had so many friends.' She had said the same thing for hours. 'And, Calum, you look that smart in your new clothes!'

Niall had brought some of his outgrown clothes for Calum to wear. Three years ago, he had been the same size as Calum was now, and the smaller boy wore tough jeans and a really neat sweat-shirt, blue with a hood. Calum looked better than Josh had ever seen him, happier as well. At half-past ten, sitting next to Josh in the pony cart, he admitted the truth.

'I'll tell you, Josh, it's made me think how lucky I am. Mairi was right. We only lost things. My mam and dad are safe. No one was hurt at all. And I'm fair delighted to be staying with you and your mam and dad and Mrs Ros. She's a grand cook, your granny.'

Josh studied Calum's thin, twitchy face. 'You're tougher than you look. A bit like Niall. I'm glad you're staying with us, Calum. It'll be great. You can ride my bike any time you want.'

'That would be grand. And your dad's a fine one for jokes. He knows more than I do.'

Josh had wondered how a bird could choose someone to throw the St Domhnall doll. At eleven o'clock he found out. All the boys stood in a circle in the field behind the bicycle sheds. In the middle, the teachers scattered bird seed and bits of sardine. It stank something awful. With Niall pale and nervous on his right, Calum bright red on his left, Josh was determined to act like a real gang boss. He took his hat off and slid it under his belt. Anyway, if birds were going to flap around him, his hat was safer off his head.

At exactly eleven o'clock, Mr Cashel took an old biscuit tin from Janet Doinnean. He spoke in Gaelic and Niall translated into Josh's ear.

'On this day, long ago, St Domhnall made friends with the birds on Feannag Ness. We call on the birds to choose a new St Domhnall and be his friends for this year.'

Mr Cashel had a good voice for making Gaelic speeches. When he had finished, he lifted the tin and shook it.

'It's full of stones,' Calum whispered. 'You can hear it for miles.'

'Birds come for the food and we wait until one pecks a lad's shoe,' Niall said. 'If no one gets pecked, the Council measure who's closest to where a bird fed. Then it looks a wee bit daft.'

'Wheesht, now!' Mr Cashel stopped shaking the tin. 'Birds are up!'

Josh peered at the white and black dots circling overhead. Around the field, parents and friends waited. Triona was there, and Mairi. Not Fearchas, however, and Josh wondered if the old man would ever return to Roncamas.

A gull swooped and attacked a sardine. A starling followed. Birds fell from the sky in a squabbling hail of feather and beak.

'Look at that!' Calum hissed. 'That big gull's going to Seoras! Ach, no, we canna have Seoras for saint! That would be too daft for words.'

Seoras winced and wiggled both feet until the bird flapped away.

Josh glanced at his watch. Quarter-past eleven. 'This is boring.'

'Wheest!' Calum scowled at him. 'Give it time.'

'I can't stand much . . . Wow!'

The birds exploded out of the circle, clattering in all directions.

'Wow! Stampede! What scared them?'

No one replied and Josh cricked his neck to look upwards. High in colourless space, a dark speck spiralled down. Growing larger. Fatter. Josh thought it was a big crow. With a squawk and a rattle of wings, it bounced onto the grass. Around the circle, boys gasped and exchanged frightened glances. Mr Cashel craned over a boy's shoulders to see.

'Ach, my word!' Calum pointed at the black bird. 'I canna believe it!'

'What's up?' Josh peered harder at the bird. 'Calum?'

'It's the crow with the silver beak. Just like in the story of St Domhnall.'

A silver beak? Oh yeah? Josh watched the bird plod over the grass. He remembered that rooks had grey beaks. So, it was a rook, not a crow.

'Ach, my word!' Calum gasped and prodded Josh with his elbow. 'It's coming this way.'

Josh did not hear him. That bird plodding towards him had a real – a real metal-glittering – a real silver beak! It was the bird from the boat! The one that had smacked Morag in the face, then appeared on the island everywhere Josh looked. Something about its eyes made Josh remember.

'It's the bird that saw you drown! Niall!' Niall was not listening. 'It can't be real. It's a set-up. Someone's painted its beak.'

But it was not paint. It was metal. Silver. And it was the bird Josh had flown with, looking down through its eyes to see Niall almost die.

The bird bounded faster, not bothering to even sniff at the sardines. It hopped straight to Niall and pecked his foot. At the other side of the circle, Mr Cashel nodded, as if he had expected this all along.

Niall flinched as the bird gave him another hard peck. In total silence. Not one boy whispered or giggled or moved. Niall's knees buckled and he sank to the bird's level.

'Not me. You dinna want me . . .'

Josh found his voice. 'Of course it wants you!'

'No . . .' Niall shivered. 'I'm no strong enough.'

The bird gave an ear-rattling shriek and flew at Niall's face, beating him with its wings. Black feathers snapped, skewering his pale hair. A final scream and the crow flapped hard. Within thirty seconds, it had vanished.

The silence shattered with cheers and whistles and clapping hands. Josh dragged Niall to his feet.

'Man, that was just grand!' Calum laughed. 'I'm that pleased for you, Niall! Look, there's your mam and dad coming! They're grinning fit to burst!'

Niall nodded, numb.

Josh shook his arm. 'Come on, Niall. All you've got to do is stay alive till Thursday. It could have been Seoras. You wouldn't want Seoras for the job, would you?'

'I would not!' Niall sighed. 'But it should be a dark-haired lad. St Domhnall was Celtic, small and dark like Calum and Mairi.'

Josh had to step back as people hurried to shake Niall's hand and his mum and dad hugged him. For the second time in two days, something slid past Josh's memory before he could grab it. The last time had been when the post office burned and he stared down from the mountain. He had seen something . . . This time, it was to do with Niall not being dark. Someone had said how strange it was, Niall not being dark. Seeing the fierce pride on Mairi's face wiped everything else away. She looked as if she would cry, any minute, she was so pleased Niall had been picked. Josh patted her shoulder and she smiled at him.

'Now, you'll all come to the Worm for lunch?' Ailsa lifted Niall into the air and he giggled. 'I'm that glad, Niall! We couldn't have a finer lad for our saint! You'll all come back now?'

In the end, even Mairi joined the celebrations. It was a

jolly meal, everyone laughing and joking. Only after the last crumb had been eaten did the conversation change, back to the burning of the post office.

'The thing is, if it was sabotage, who'd do it?' Nathan waved Josh quiet. 'I know you think it was the Detritex men, but why would they hit the post office? No one knew it was empty . . . Unless someone heard you on the radio, Josh?'

'Iain was outside, all the time . . . Oh shoot!'

'What?' His dad stared at him. 'Josh?'

'I should have thought! I mean, if they had their mail brought in by a special boat, they wouldn't use a public radio, would they?' Josh groaned. 'Dad, there's a radio at Falamh Taigh. I saw the aerial from Beinn Dubh and I forgot. The Detritex men have been going to the coast-guards, pretending that they had to use the radio there. But they had one of their own, all the time. They could listen in to all our calls. They'd have heard us, when I told you Calum saw their mail. And they'd know the post office was empty. I bet . . .' Josh shivered. 'I bet they were so mad with Calum for spying on their mail, they waited until the post office was empty and set fire to it. Morag hinted that something would happen. And that was it. They burned the post office down because we looked at their mail.'

His dad nodded slowly. 'Hector, you said the fire melted the radio. How about a fire bomb in the radio room?'

'This is serious,' Hector said. 'Folk could have died fighting that fire.'

'Morag wouldn't care. She nearly pushed me over-board. And she stood in the road, waiting for our bikes.' Josh shuddered. 'Niall could have cracked his skull on the bridge-post and she laughed about it.'

Fiona stood up. 'Niall, you never told us!'

'I didn't want to worry you,' Niall said. 'She hinted something bad was going to happen. She's warning us off.'

'Ach, my good Lord!' Fiona sat down again. 'That wicked, wicked woman! And we've not a scrap of proof. It's no crime to own a radio.'

'Look, I know I'm not on the Council, but I think we should meet these people. Let's get them over here and ask what they're playing at.' Nathan looked around the table and, one by one, everyone nodded.

The Detritex men agreed to a meeting at three that afternoon. So, Falamh Taigh would be empty. Josh thought he could get there in about forty minutes on his bike.

8 Josh in Trouble

At twenty past two, Josh took Calum to one side. It was unfair to pick on Calum and Josh felt bad about it. Calum was so anxious not to be in the way, he would agree to anything.

'Calum, I'm going for a ride . . .' He forced a smile. 'You don't mind, do you?'

'Ach, of course not, Josh.'

'If anyone asks, I'm watching the boats.' All lies, but Josh kept his nice smile. 'See you later.'

Of course, it was all very well telling Calum lies. Try telling lies to a small, angry seagull. Josh had only peddled to the crossroads when Spog attacked him.

'Hey! Pack it in!' He swatted her away. 'Spog! Clear off!' Spog clawed his jacket. Then she lifted her tail and squirted white bird-stuff down his zip.

'Oh, thanks a lot! Look, I'm only . . .' Josh glared at her. 'I'm only talking to a bird! Push off!'

Spog squealed and flew after him, only giving up when he passed the Triathan house. Muttering, Josh cleaned his jacket with a tissue. The white mess stank of fish.

'Great! If they don't see me coming, they'll smell me! Thanks a lot, Spog.'

The only place Josh could hide was in the trees near Loch Darach. He got there two minutes before the car swept past. Gasping, he waited until it was almost out of sight, then bobbed up to examine the back seat. Morag was there. The house would be empty.

The gate to Falamh Taigh stood open. Like most island homes, the house had no high fence, just a tumbled stone wall an ant could have hopped over. Josh pushed his bike between the gate-posts, into the muddy mess of Morag's garden. Slow drizzle sifted down, dripping from his nose.

'Right.' He turned his hat around. 'Get looking.'

First, he walked around the house, peering at windows. Curtains blocked every one until he reached the back. Wobbling on tiptoe, he squinted through the narrow gap between the drapes.

Morag's study, Josh decided. Dusty bottles spilled out of the bookcases in layers. A quarry for books. If he really stretched . . . A sheep's skull gazed at him from empty eye-sockets. Beside it, an old sword glinted, wrapped in snake-skin. Josh tried to force the window open but it was locked. So was the back door. And the front.

'Shoot!' Josh kicked the front step. 'Hey, wait a minute . . .'

He ran his fingers over the doorstep. Scratches. Heart thudding, Josh examined every window-sill for scratches. The study had a whole tangle, clawed into the stone wall as high as his shoulders.

'OK, so how come no tracks?' Josh was no boy scout, but he had been careful to check the path for tracks. What sort of cat could scratch solid stone but leave no tracks in mud? 'This is stupid!'

If Morag was up to something, she was doing it in the house. Apart from all that bone-throwing.

'I wonder . . .?' Josh wondered why she had chosen that particular spot to mess about with her bones. 'Unless it's special.'

The steep path along Falamburn had a fine selection of footprints, skidding over rocks, down into a gorge full of waterfalls. Gorse bushes hung over the edge, spooky in the fine mist of rain. All Josh heard was falling water. The spray drenched him, spotting his specs, and mud oozed into his trainers. At the bottom of the gorge, stepping stones . . .

A better path followed this side of the burn. It passed the tolleun then divided, one branch west down Loch Darach, the other taking the wooden bridge back over Falamburn, eastwards into the trees. Josh perched on top of the mound of stones. Below him lay Morag's magic circle of burned grass. Within a few metres were the fork in the path, the bridge crossing the water, the burn itself dividing earth from earth. Three sets of meeting places.

'That's it. That's why she does her funny stuff here.'

Josh crawled around the tolleun, searching for clues . . . Like that faint path climbing the west side of the gorge! Excited now, he pushed through the wet grass. And a bird exploded from nowhere, almost into his face. A crow. Josh stared at it. The crow with the silver beak flapped up from the grass and nodded its head, squawking. Telling him something.

'What?' He ducked just in time. 'All right! I'll look!'

But the bird flew back, nearly smacking him in the teeth. Three times. Then it soared upwards, leaving him kneeling in the grass, breathless and shaking.

The hole was invisible from the path and Josh would have missed it if the crow had not appeared. Fringed with grass, it dropped into pitch black nothing. When he closed his eyes, he heard the distant sound of water – drips falling from a great height and a deeper sound, water running over stone. Why had the crow wanted him to see it? He could not have fallen down it, it was too far from the path. Why did the bird want him to know about a hole in the ground?

Josh followed the path again, north between gorse and high rocks towards Loch Falamh. When it suddenly opened out, he stopped. A muddy clearing, pitted with bootprints, stretched for some three metres. In the middle sat a heavy, wooden lid, padlocked and chained.

'It's a well.' Josh kicked the woodwork. 'This is brand new . . .'

'That it is, laddie.'

The man stepped from behind a clump of gorse. One of the Detritex men – all flash suit, slicked-back hair, a big gold ring on his little finger. He must have been waiting.

'Oh . . . Hi.' Josh swallowed. 'I was just . . .'

'Nosing around, is what you were just.' The man walked towards him. 'I thought you'd find your way here. With a nose like that, you're a grand one for sniffing around.'

Josh had only looked for Morag on the back seat of the car. He had seen a man's head above the driving seat and not bothered with the passenger side. A big mistake. The crow had been telling him to get out of there. He should have listened to the crow.

'Come here, you! Now!'

Josh spun on his heel and ran for it. Three strides and the man rugby-tackled him, slamming him onto the swampy path. Josh's hat fell off.

'I said come here!' The man twisted Josh's arms. 'Get up! Now!'

The man dragged him, struggling, to the wooden lid and threw him on top of it. Josh's head bounced off the concrete edge. 'Now, dinna move!'

The man's face was too close. Josh saw it too clearly, every bit of bristle he had missed with his razor, the pasty-wet skin, sharp nose, crooked front tooth.

'Do you know what you're lying on, fat guts?' The man jabbed Josh in the stomach. 'It's an auld well. A fine, deep, rat-infested well. And the lid's that thick, it's soundproof. I'll tell you, laddie, I've been down there. You can scream fit to bust and no one will hear you.'

Josh tried to sit up and the man slapped him across the mouth. It knocked his glasses off and the man grinned and smashed them under his expensive shoe.

'Now, you little black bastard . . . My boss is a wee touch squeamish. He wants no one hurt. Now me, I dinna mind the sight of blood. Especially with the money Morag's paying us to finish this place. She'd give it away, if she could. But she canna give it away, it's protected by having birds here. So, she's paying us to persuade our bosses *they* want it. And then this whole place will die . . . So you be off the island by Thursday or very nasty things might happen.' He grinned and jabbed Josh's stomach again. 'Pubs burn as fast as post offices. Or your dad could have a wee accident . . .'

'Don't you dare touch my dad!' Josh sat up.

'Or what?' The man back-handed him, his gold ring splitting Josh's lip. 'Morag should have fixed you on the boat. Or you could break a leg . . . Out here, on your own . . . They'd no find you for days.'

He grabbed Josh's ears, one in each hand, and twisted. 'Now, say after me . . . I won't tell anyone about this.'

Josh wriggled and kicked but the man only twisted harder. Tears ran up Josh's nose. He felt the skin under his ears stretching. 'I won't . . . tell . . .'

'And you'll be away from here by Thursday.' He twisted and tore the skin. 'Say it!'

'I'll go away! Oww!'

'So, this is our secret. Or I'll come and find you. And you'll be very, very sorry.'

The man dropped Josh's head, grinning when it thudded against the wood. He looked pleased with himself.

Josh rolled onto his stomach, sobbing, trying not to, wanting to be sick, not wanting to wet his pants. When the man stamped his boot on the well lid, Josh sprawled onto his feet and ran.

'Dinna forget your bike, will you?'

Josh lay between two banks of heather for twenty minutes, curled up and crying while the rain fell on his face. He was sick, once, and his insides had turned to water. Shaking, teeth rattling, he washed his hands and face in Falamburn then staggered, rubber-kneed, all around Loch Falamh and back to the road. His bike was filthy, trodden into the mud, and he squinted because he had no glasses. His feet would not lift onto the pedals, so he pushed the bike. When he heard the car coming out of the fog, he burrowed into the grass like a rabbit. Only after Beinn Dubh could he slither onto the saddle and he fell off twice before he got home.

'Josh!' Ishbel dropped her cup on the kitchen floor. 'Heaven help us, laddie! What have you done to yourself? Josh, pet!'

'Fell off my bike. And I lost my hat.' Josh's face twisted and he stood there bawling.

'Wheesht!' Ishbel hugged him, stroking his face. 'Wheesht, my bairn! Are you hurt bad? There's blood down your neck . . .'

Josh gulped and shook his head.

'Nathan! Nathan! Josh has hurt himself . . . You poor wee soul! You're shaking.'

Josh heard feet running. He could not look and crushed his face into Ishbel's chest. Her buttons caught his nose.

101

'What's the matter?' Calum's voice, frightened. 'Josh!'

'He's fallen off his bike. His face is bruised something awful. And his poor wee ears are bleeding.'

'His ears?' Nathan tried to ease Josh into his own arms. 'Josh, let me see. Come on, Josh. I want to see.'

Josh clung to Ishbel as hard as he could. He did not want anyone to see him. Not to see his face. Then he started to feel dizzy. Faint.

'I've got to lie down . . . I feel really awful.' Ishbel hurried him upstairs. 'I'm sorry, Ishbel.'

'There's nothing to be sorry about. You're in shock, my pet.' She helped him into his room, holding him while he pulled his muddy jeans down. 'You'll be just fine. You're home, now. You'll be grand, in the morning.'

'No I won't!' He glared up at her. 'I won't! I hate it here! I want to go home! I want to go back to London!'

After that, everything blurred. Josh remembered collapsing in tears, his dad picking him up, the jeans still around his ankles, and putting him on the bed. Ailsa tucked him up with hot water bottles and Josh squirmed away from her. When he fell asleep, he moaned and cried, remembering the man's face.

It sounded like a nice morning – a light breeze and birds singing. Spog had pecked his window for an hour, then given up. Josh lay very still, watching the clock. It was time for school and he flinched when the door opened.

'Josh?' Calum peered into the room. 'Are you no getting up? Are you still feeling bad?'

'I'm not going to school.' Josh pulled the sheets over his face. 'Go away, Calum.'

'All right, Josh. I'll go.'

★

102

People kept trying to talk to him. His dad looked upset and confused. Ishbel cried. Only Ailsa was calm and firm, making Josh eat lunch. He stayed in bed all day, waiting for the gang to come. He would refuse to see them, hide under the bed-clothes until they went home. He started to cry again, because he was a coward. A stinking, rotten coward.

At five o'clock, someone tapped on the door.

'Josh? Can we come in?' Niall's voice.

'No! Go away!'

Triona barged into the room, poodle-ears quivering. 'What happened?' She plonked down on the bed. 'Josh, what happened? Your mam's been crying, she's that worried about you.'

'Nothing happened!' Josh buried his face in the pillow. 'Go away!'

Chairs slid on the carpet and he heard the gang sit, felt their eyes on his back.

'I know it's something bad,' Niall said. 'But, Josh, we're your friends. Whatever happened, we'll help you.'

'I'm going back to London.' Josh forced himself to look up. 'That's all. I don't want you here . . . Please, Niall. Just leave me alone.'

Niall bit his lip and his fists clenched, but he nodded and started to stand.

'No you don't!' Triona jerked Niall back onto his chair. 'We dinna go until Josh tells us what happened. Josh, we're in this together. You've got to tell us . . . Or we'll no talk to you again.'

Josh gaped at her. Her face was so red, her white brows looked false. Like Father Christmas. But she was not giving him a Father Christmas smile. Josh had expected everyone to be nice to him, not to threaten him.

'I mean it, Josh. I promise I do.'

Calum sighed. 'I'm sorry, Josh. I promise, as well. You've got to tell us what happened.'

Mairi nodded. 'Promise.'

Everyone looked at Niall. Triona caught his arm and dug her nails into it. 'Niall! Go on!'

'Tree, I canna promise.' Niall shook his head, sadly. 'It's not something I'd do, sending folk to Coventry.'

Calum had leaned closer to the bed. 'Seoras once twisted my ears nearly off my head. That's where I bled, as well. You canna do that to yourself, falling off your bike.'

Josh touched his poor ears. The day before, Ailsa had put iodine on them, which had stung like acid. He could feel the scabs.

Niall groaned. 'Oh, Josh! You went to Falamh Taigh! The other Detritex man caught you!'

'I'm not telling you! He might hurt my dad!' Josh's face crumpled and he tried to hide it with his hands. His voice rattled. 'He made me cry! I was so scared! If I stay here, he'll do something awful.'

'Do you think we'd let him hurt you again?' Triona glowered at him. 'Me and Calum and Mairi and Niall and all our families? Mairi would scratch his eyes out if he came near you.'

Mairi nodded. 'Josh. You brave.'

Brave? Josh felt better. Surprised, he wiped his eyes and looked at Tree's big, ugly face, Mairi's thin, wild one. 'He said he'd burn the Worm down, as well . . . or hurt my dad. If I wasn't off the island by Thursday.'

Calum propped his feet on the bed. 'So, it's all about Thursday? You missed the meeting, Josh. Mr King was here with Morag. He admitted Detritex want the island to dump waste on. My guess is they'll try to spoil Tilleun

Sealmath.'

If King had been here, the man hurting Josh had been MacNeil. Josh was never going to forget MacNeil's face but, now that the gang was with him, he could think about it without crying.

'What good would that do?' Josh sat up. He felt fine. 'I mean, it would upset people . . .'

'It would more than upset people.' Niall's eyes widened. 'It's when we ask the birds to stay for another year. Maybe Morag thinks the birds will leave . . .'

Calum nudged Josh with his foot. 'Josh, you canna run because of those men.'

'It's revenge you want, Josh.' Triona bounced up and down on his bed, angrily. 'The gang canna be scared away like that.'

Josh slumped back. 'I'm not in the gang, any more . . . Even if I stay here.'

'Don't talk daft!' Triona snapped. 'Of course you're staying! Of course you're in the gang!'

'I can't be the Boss, anyway. Not after he made me cry . . . He made me say things . . .' Josh forced himself to speak. 'He made me promise not to tell anyone. Niall, you'll be Boss, now.'

'I will not!' Niall gasped. 'Josh, you're the Boss! None of us would have gone to Falamh Taigh, alone. And the Boss has to think what's best for the whole gang. I canna do that.'

Calum nodded. 'It's true, Josh. Niall's too nice to boss us around. Triona's too bossy already. And Mairi and I would be useless. It has to be you.'

Josh swallowed. 'You still want me to be Boss?'

'Of course we do!' Triona stood up. 'Now, that's settled. You're staying, you're the Boss and we're going to make Morag right sorry!'

'She burned my home, Josh.' Calum stood as well. 'We canna let her get away with that.'

'At least we know what she wants.' Niall frowned at the carpet. 'To turn the island into a stinking heap of waste. She hates us that much, she's crazy with it.'

'From now on, we've got to watch each other's backs.' Josh swung out of bed and padded to the table for his spare specs. Putting them on made him feel even better, like starting again with a clean slate. 'Mairi, you'd better stay with Tree until Thursday . . . Is that OK?'

Triona nodded. 'Fine by me. Mairi can try all my frocks on and my mam will have a grand time doing her hair.'

'Calum's with me and we'll meet Niall at the crossroads every morning.' Josh's mind had started to work again. He sat on the window-sill, giving orders, loving every minute. 'Never leave your houses empty. I'll get Willy-John to keep an eye on the Worm. Niall, what about you?'

'We could get someone to stay, for a few days . . .'

'Your grandad can look after himself, Mairi. No bother, there.' Josh looked at Triona. 'Tree? There's the vicarage and the church.'

'I'll tell my dad. And there's always folk in the church.'

'Right, then.' Josh waggled his toes, happily. 'And I saw something really weird, yesterday . . .'

He told them nearly everything. Somehow, he could not talk about being beaten up, not just yet. They discussed the cat scratches and the tolleun near three sets of meeting places. In two days, whatever was going to happen would be over.

'The crow with the silver beak picked Niall,' Triona said. 'I tell you, Josh, it should be our best Sealmath ever. There'll be that much good luck, Morag will run to the mainland and never come back.'

9   In the Well

Wednesday morning.

'Spog?' Josh leaned out of the window. 'What's up? Not hungry?'

The little gull prodded the bread with her beak, then paddled back up the roof. She gave him a pitiful squeak and tried to climb his pyjama jacket.

'No you don't! Go on, hop it!' Josh watched her glide away. 'Hey! Green sky!'

Calum peered around the bedroom door. 'Josh? Are you up and ready?'

'Hey, Calum. Have you looked outside?'

'Aye, I have. The sky's fair drained of colour.'

'It's green.'

'Well . . .' Calum pulled a face. 'I was hoping I'd dreamt the colour. The milk's soured in the fridge. And Willy-John says the ponies are all sweated up. It's an ill start to the day.'

The butter had gone off, as well, and the cheese smelt like feet. In the hotel yard, some very miserable birds huddled together, not bothering to eat or fly. Even Goath buried his head in his wings and waddled away.

'Josh, look at this.' Niall waited, tall and pale, beside the tolleun. 'Touch the stones.'

Josh winced. 'They're cold!'

'The other tolleun's the same.' Niall gazed at the sky.

'This green makes me sick to the stomach! And there's precious little in my stomach, with the whole fridge turned bad.'

Triona and Mairi waited at the church gate.

'I canna believe this sky!' Triona said. 'And Mairi had bad dreams all night.'

'Running. All wet.' Mairi shivered. 'Bad sky.'

Worrying about the sky and Spog and the ice-cold tolleun, Josh did not think about being away from school the day before. When he saw Seoras, he expected the usual jokes about the gang. He had a few to throw right back. Like, where did Seoras buy his shoes? From a plumber? Stuff like that. Instead, Seoras pointed to Josh's swollen ears.

'Did you catch your ears in the spokes, then? Shame it wasn't your face.'

Calum sighed. 'Ach, this is too much. Now I'll tell you, Seoras, from now on, every time you hurt one of us, you'll have to fight the rest, straight after.'

'Is that right, now?' Seoras lifted his fist under Calum's nose. 'And should that scare me, shrimp-face?'

'Well, you're fair terrified of Mairi. And if you dinna move your fist, I'll give you such a thump, you'll land in the harbour.'

Seoras grinned at Josh, Triona, Mairi. Then at Niall. 'Now that I canna believe. Niall Triathan fighting back, for a change? You'd no have the nerve!'

'The world's fair aching with wonders, Seoras. The sky's green as grass. Maybe I'd find the nerve, if I had to.' Niall smiled, sweetly. 'I'll tell you what. You leave us be and we'll leave you be.'

The bell rang for the first lesson and Seoras turned away. 'You're daft, the lot of you!'

Josh grinned. 'Calum, that was magic! You really stood up to him.'

'Aye, I did. It was about time.'

So, Calum had stood up to Seoras. Mairi was talking, Triona was nicer to people. There was only Niall to toughen up. Unfortunately, Mr Cashel had decided to pick on him. Every quarter of an hour, he called Niall out of the class to carry this, move that. When he appeared, again, in the third lesson, Josh groaned.

'Niall, tell him to pick on somebody else!'

'He's the Principal, Josh. I can hardly tell him to go stuff himself. He says I'm not to think I'm special, just because I'm throwing the Domhnall doll.' Niall pulled his sweat-shirt off. Underneath, his shirt shone soap-powder white. 'I'm just that knackered, heaving auld books around.'

Niall followed Mr Cashel to the school book-cupboard, trying to look eager and helpful.

'Start on the floor and sort the books into piles.' Cashel opened the door. 'There's a light inside. Close the door so no one runs into it.'

'Fine, sir.'

'When you're done, I'll open the windows and clear this stink. Now, get started. You dinna want to miss your lunch.'

Niall waited until Cashel had gone, then slammed the door. 'Miss my lunch! You auld hypocrite! And if there's anyone feels less special, I canna think who! Ach, it's unfair.'

And Cashel was right, it did stink in there. Eyes watering, Niall pulled a heap of books onto the floor and sorted the reds into piles.

'First English Reader . . .' He coughed and swallowed. 'This stink is something awful.'

When he turned, the store-room spun around him and he overbalanced, clutching the door handle. The door was locked. Someone had locked him in. Little black specks floated in the air. Confused, not understanding what was wrong, Niall heard the breath gasp into his chest, the blood thud in his ears. He slid down the wall, onto the floor. It felt like nothing. He could not feel anything. He tried to yell but his voice had died. He could not move. The air turned hot and dark and sticky, and he fainted.

'Niall!' Mairi shot out of her chair. 'Niall! Niall!'

Josh caught her and she tried to bite him, fighting to be free.

'Mairi!' Janet ran to help. 'Whatever's the matter, lass?'

'Niall!' Mairi punched Josh in the ribs. Tears ran down her face. 'Gone! Niall gone!'

Janet frowned. 'Where is Niall, Josh?'

'He was helping Mr Cashel.' Badly frightened, Josh clung to Mairi's sleeve. 'It's all right, Mairi . . . It's all right . . .'

'Gone!' Mairi fell against his chest, howling.

'Mam, I'll look after her.' Triona pulled Mairi into her arms. 'Come on, Mairi. Come and sit down.'

'Good lass, Tree.' Janet frowned. 'Josh, you'd best find Niall as quickly as you can . . . Calum, you too. He canna be far away.'

Someone had opened every window in the corridor and a sluggish breeze flowed through. Josh and Calum searched every classroom, every cupboard, the canteen, the boiler-room, everywhere. All they found was a funny stink that reminded Josh of the locusts his old school used in biology. What had locusts to do with anything? Ten minutes later, he knocked at Mr Cashel's door.

'Come in.'

Josh cleared his throat. 'Please, sir. We're looking for Niall Triathan.'

'Is he no back in class?' Cashel stood up, frowning. 'It's taking him a deal of time to tidy the books.'

'He isn't anywhere,' Josh said.

Mr Cashel's eyes narrowed. 'As you can see, he's no hiding under my desk. And if he's left school during lessons, I'll be after his hide.'

'He wouldn't!' Josh winced. 'Sir, Niall would never do that.'

'Then he's somewhere in school. He's no the Invisible Man.'

Mr Cashel beside them, Josh and Calum went over the whole school again. Nothing. When Cashel stalked into Class Three, he was fuming.

'Mrs Doinnean, we appear to have lost Niall Triathan.'

Mairi shrieked. 'All dark! Niall!'

Cashel glared at her. 'Be quiet!'

'She's frightened, sir. And so am I.' Janet put her chalk firmly on her desk. 'We should start searching straight away.'

'For a boy playing truant?'

'For a boy gone missing.' Janet met Cashel's eyes and a very Triona-type scowl crinkled her brow. 'Niall would no play truant.'

'I was working him a touch hard . . .' Cashel sighed. 'Aye, very well then. But I'm sure he's safe at home.'

By three o'clock that afternoon, the whole of Roncamas was out looking for Niall. Just to confuse everyone, Morag and the Detritex men had the perfect alibi. When

111

Niall disappeared, they had been with his mum and dad at the hospital, discussing a donation to the X-Ray Fund. There was no trace of Niall in or anywhere around the school.

'He was worried about tomorrow and Cashel was getting at him,' Calum said, 'but he'd no run away.'

'We know that!' Josh tried not to look at Mairi, curled up on his bed like a dead squirrel. She clung to Niall's sweat-shirt, sobbing. Josh groaned. 'If Morag hadn't been at the hospital!'

'Ach, it's ridiculous!' Calum punched the air. 'I canna think at all.'

Josh snorted. 'The Council didn't want police spoiling tomorrow but it's well spoilt now. What if Niall doesn't show up?'

'They'll pick another lad.' Triona stalked around the room, kicking things. 'I canna imagine what will happen tomorrow.'

'Birds not come.' Mairi sniffed and uncurled slightly. 'Wrong boy throw doll. Birds not come. Never. Go away.'

'I should have known!' Josh lost his temper with himself. 'They wanted to ruin Sealmath. Grabbing Niall is a great way of ruining it.'

'Man, it's driving me crazy!' Calum butted his head on the window. 'There's no way Niall could vanish like that . . .' He stopped and stared. 'That's the Detritex mail-boat. What's it doing?'

The boat bounced gently against the pier and a man jumped on board. He had a suitcase in each hand and would have fallen if the sailors hadn't caught him. He nodded and they cast off, the boat swinging into the harbour.

'Cashel!' Josh banged on the window. 'It is! He's running for it! Locusts!' He banged the window, again, wished it would break. 'He's one of them! He works for Detritex!'

Triona stared at him. 'What are you blethering on about? Locusts?'

'I thought he didn't want a black kid in his school. I thought that was why he was so funny with me.'

'But he's done nothing to run from, Josh.'

'He has! All those windows open to get rid of the smell! We had locusts at my last school. We'd knock them out with ether. And that's what I could smell.' Josh groaned. 'We searched the whole school. But not Cashel's car. Niall couldn't yell for help if he was out cold.'

Mairi sat up. 'Drug?'

'Drugged! The store-room's right next to the car-park door. No one would see Cashel dump Niall in the boot.' Josh met Mairi's eyes. 'Mairi, do you always know where Niall is? Even when he's asleep?'

'Sometimes . . .' She wet her lips with her tongue, forcing the words out. 'Like dreaming . . .'

'Right.' Josh sat next to her. 'Think about him now.'

'No . . . Dark.' She hugged Niall's sweat-shirt to her chest. 'I try and try . . . Dark, Josh.'

'Can you hear water?'

Mairi gasped. 'Water! Yes!'

'MacNeil wasn't supposed to beat me up, he won't have told Morag I was there.' Josh stood up, angrier than he had ever been in his life. 'They've put Niall down the well! With the rats and all that water. He'll be scared to death!'

'Folk are spread all around the island,' Calum said. 'It'll take hours to find everyone.'

'We're not waiting. Fearchas told me, I've got to look

113

after Niall.' Josh looked at his three friends. 'There's a way down Morag doesn't know about. Niall's crow showed me. I knew it was trying to tell me something. It wanted me to know how we could get Niall out again. We'll lower Calum down . . .'

'Me?' Calum's jaw dropped. 'Why me?'

'Because you're the smallest. We'll need a bicycle each and ropes and torches . . .'

'Take Niall home . . .' Mairi held Josh's hand. 'Take him . . . Liath Bealach. Grandad help us.'

Josh nodded. 'And tomorrow we'll drive into Ronca-mas and Niall will throw the doll over the cliff.' He stood up and held his hand out. They all knew what he wanted, all put their own hands on his. 'OK, gang. Let's do it!'

Even peddling hard, they did not reach Loch Darach until six. The light fell sickly yellow and the sky pressed down on them, green marbled with grey cloud. Half an hour later, they crawled to the hole in the grass. And Josh knelt on something flat and black and leathery.

'Hey!' He picked it up. 'I've found my hat!'

'So that's all right, then.' Triona pushed him forwards. 'Now we can get on with finding Niall.'

Calum tore the grass away from the hole, leaving a rough circle of rock. Within the circle hid whispering, rippling darkness.

Josh leaned over and bellowed. 'Niall! Niall, can you hear me?'

Mairi nearly knocked him head-first into the hole, kneeling all over him. 'Niall! Niall!'

Everyone waited. And, far below, a faint voice answered.

'You took your time.'

114

Josh laughed with relief. 'We're coming, Niall. Are you all right?'

'Are you serious?' His voice shivered. 'I'm frozen stiff . . . I canna see a thing . . . It's like a dream, Josh. Where am I?'

'In Morag's well. Calum's coming down to you.'

'There are rats, you know.' Niall coughed, then sounded slightly stronger. 'Josh, I canna feel my hands and feet. I doubt I can walk.'

Their first attempt at lowering Calum ended with him screaming and clawing back out of the gap. The rope had bitten deep into his ribs. Padded with every woolly jumper in the group and Josh's favourite jacket, he tried again.

'Man, this is ridiculous! I might not fit in the hole.' But he shrugged to the edge, gripping the rope at shoulder height. 'And if you drop me, I'll no speak to you again.'

Josh grinned. 'You'd be splat like a fly on a windscreen, Calum. You wouldn't be saying much to anyone.'

'That makes me feel just grand, Josh.' Calum slithered into the hole. 'Torch, Mairi.'

Calum opened his mouth and Mairi put the torch in sideways. He nodded, closed his eyes and vanished.

Calum hung from the rope like a hooked fish. After thirty seconds, he opened one eye. Deep rock spun around him, a vertical tube slimed with old water gone black and rotten. Mouldy cold sucked into his chest. Water dripped onto his face. Drip. Plip. Plup. Another thirty seconds and he released the rope, shining the torch downwards.

'I can see water!'

The tunnel widened in jerks as he swung lower. Wider, again. Gone! He dangled in black space. On the right, the torch-beam found a narrow ledge.

'There's a ledge, Josh. I'm going to swing over to it.'

Calum kicked his legs and soon had a nice momentum behind him. The ledge widened around a ridge of rock. In the other direction, the cave became a passage filled almost to the roof with water. The underground stream gushed under Calum's feet, black and oily.

Up on the ground, Josh, Triona and Mairi clung to the rope with all their strength. Josh's teeth ached, he clenched them so hard. Triona's face shone red. Mairi snarled and dug her feet into the grass. Each swing of the rope jerked it harder between their fingers. They were all strong, but not that . . .

Calum ran out of rope at the furthest edge of his swing, yelled, and felt it whip free. Triona screamed but he was already falling. He hit the wall and sat in a soggy mess of leaves, both feet dragging in the water.

'Ach, my word!' His knees trembled and he felt sick. The rope lay there, useless with no one holding the other end. 'Now that hurt . . .'

'Calum! Are you all right?'

'A wee bit bruised about the backside, Josh . . . But I think there's a quick way out. Niall will no like it.'

Calum crawled along the ledge, not enjoying the slippery leaves at all. Easy to slip into the water. He peered around the rocky ridge. Niall lay a dozen metres away, tied wrists to ankles on a pile of sacks. His white shirt glowed in the torchlight. The men had blindfolded him as well, and that was pure spite. It was pitch black down there anyway. Calum knelt on something soft that squealed and jumped into the water.

'Rats,' Niall said. He tried to lift his head. 'Is that you, Calum?'

'Aye, it is. Ach, those bastards! They could have left you more comfortable than this.'

'A few cushions would have been nice.' Niall coughed, painfully. 'I've been screaming for hours. I dinna care for rats.'

Calum could think of nothing to say. Quivering with anger, he shone his torch on Niall's back. The poor lad's hands looked like plastic, swollen and dead white, blue around the nails. Calum touched one and winced.

'You're like ice! And sopping wet! Here, let's get that blindfold off.'

Even the blindfold oozed cold water, dripped on from the roof.

Niall managed a stiff grin. 'It's grand to see you, Calum.' Then his bruised face twisted and he jammed his eyes shut. 'I thought I was here for good. What time is it?'

'Gone six.'

'Is it still Wednesday?'

'Ach, Niall!' Calum stared at the cuts and bruises on Niall's face. Someone had had a grand time thumping him. 'Aye, it's still Wednesday.'

In silence, Calum worked his penknife on the hard ropes. There had been no reason to tie them so tight and Calum swore to himself, hating whoever had done it. Cowards, he thought. When the first rope snapped, Niall's hands dropped like stones.

'Now your feet. Try to wiggle your toes.'

'Calum, I canna feel my toes.'

The last rope sawed apart, Calum propped Niall against the cave wall. For a moment, both boys listened to the drip-drop, swoosh, the squeaks as rats dived into the dark water.

Niall cleared his throat. 'Calum, you know you're dragging a great lump of rope behind you? I'm trying to be brave, Calum, but if you've lost the way back up, that makes two of us in trouble.'

'Can you wiggle your toes, Niall? Can you move your arms, now?'

'They're frozen solid.' Niall's shoulders slid up the rock but his arms flapped, uselessly. 'And you've no answered my question.'

'I came through a wee hole in the roof. There's another way out but you'll no like it.'

Niall's eyes closed again. 'Calum . . . Just get me out of here. I dinna care how. I'm too cold. I'm too near the water. I've about had enough.'

Calum lifted Niall's hands and started to clap them together. The fingers got in the way, stiff and wet and horrible. 'We'll have to swim for it.'

'What!'

'In yon wee river . . . I think it flows into Falamburn.'

'Calum . . .' Niall stared at him, horrified. 'I can scarcely sit straight.'

'I'll life-save you.' Calum forced a grin. 'You know I'm a grand swimmer.'

Niall just looked at him, then tugged his hands free. This time, his arms shuddered up in front of him but the elbows swung like broken wings. In the poor torch-glow, he could have been a black and white photograph. There was no colour in him at all.

'We'll have to go. It's getting awful green outside.' Calum unpeeled the layers of borrowed woollies. 'All right, Niall?'

'Aye, all right!'

Calum gave Niall a last, shaky grin. 'It'll be cold in the water, mind. Hold your breath in case you go under.'

Niall flinched and nodded, slithering to the edge. Calum sat close to him, an arm around his neck.

'On three, Niall. One . . . two . . .'

They hit the water.

'Ach, God!' Niall went straight under.

Calum hauled his friend up and lay back into the current. The cold ate through his shirt. 'Man, it's cold! Are you all right, lad?'

'No.'

'Fine. Just lie back. Let's hope there's no waterfalls down here.'

Niall groaned.

Water sucked them through the rock tunnel like two peas in a drain-pipe, spinning them from wall to wall in a deafening, pitch-dark flood. If the roof came down to meet the surface of the water, they were both done for, but Calum did not want to mention that. And with this great roar in his ears, he would never hear a waterfall. He thought, suddenly, about his mam and dad and what they would feel like if he died, down here. He should have left a note.

10   Night of the Poison Cat

Josh and the others had bounded down the path to Falamburn, splashing along the bank in search of the cave mouth. Shattering water deafened them and the horrible green glow twisted the world out of shape. Josh was starting to get scared when he heard Calum's yell.

'Ach, my word!'

Two pairs of feet appeared, upside down, behind a crop of rocks and a frantic splashing erupted into the burn. Calum rose from the water like the Loch Ness monster, dragging Niall behind him.

Mairi fell on the two boys, knocking Calum flat. 'Niall!' She picked him up by the shoulders. When his eyes opened, she dropped him again.

'Mairi! Mind, you'll brain him!' Calum managed to push her away and haul Niall's legs out of the water.

Niall coughed, once, and struggled to sit up. 'Josh, you've found your hat.'

'Yeah.' Josh wondered if MacNeil had bruised Niall's face, like that. There was a cut, where a gold ring had smacked against Niall's cheekbone. 'He hit you when you were out cold!'

'Well, at least I slept through it.' Niall smiled at him. 'Dinna fret, Josh. I'll be fine.'

With Josh on one side, Triona on the other, Niall swayed onto his feet. His ankles buckled but he did not notice until he tripped over them.

'Ach, stupid feet! You'll have to drag me.'

Mairi clung to Niall's left hand, rubbing it so hard Calum thought she'd skin it bare. It was a good idea, though, and he attacked the right one.

'We'll cross Falamburn at the bridge.' Relief was making Josh light-headed. 'Try to stamp your feet, Niall. Get the blood circulating.'

Overhead, dark clouds slid together, smothering the greenish sun. If Josh had not been feeling so happy, he might have thought it was all a bit too neat, like one of those speeded-up films. It took him several, breathless minutes to notice how dark the path was suddenly. He shivered. 'Is it getting colder, or what?'

'It's getting colder.' Niall's teeth rattled. 'I'm sorry about your jacket, Josh. Calum had to leave it.'

Josh shrugged. 'It doesn't matter. Come on, Niall, try.'

'I am trying!' Niall slammed his crooked ankles onto the path. 'If you'd go slower, I might keep up with you.'

They slowed down and Niall managed to stand on his own two feet, cursing at the pain and stumbling every second step. With Triona's fist in his back, urging him forwards, he was the first to round the bend in the path.

The sky turned pitch black in one second and a wild shriek rang out. Morag Falamh leapt up, caught in the centre of her magic circle. To her left, sickly green inside, the old tolleun was the only source of light. Her face glistened, foul yellow.

'You!' Her fingers stabbed at Niall. 'You canna be here! You're in the dark, with the rats gnawing at you!'

Josh stepped forwards. And stopped. And stepped backwards, faster, standing all over Calum's feet. 'Look at that!'

The rotting-flesh stink drove Josh back, tangled up in Calum's legs. Triona had recoiled, choking, leaving Niall and Mairi alone.

'Cat.' Mairi pointed at the green-glowing cat's skeleton. 'Poison cat.'

Safe in her circle, Morag started to smile. The skeleton sat at the other side of the burnt grass, facing the path.

'It looks radioactive,' Niall said. 'Mairi, get behind me! Josh, back up, fast!'

'I am!' Josh blundered faster. 'Look at its eyes!'

Morag laughed. 'Remember them, do you? There wasn't much of a body, last time. Now you'll see the real thing.' Her face rippled with green light, speckled with spit. 'And your viking-haired friend won't call the birds. You'll no be there, Triathan!'

'Morag, dinna do it.' Niall fought Mairi behind him, putting his body between her and the glowing cat bones. 'Morag, if you say that . . .' He started to tremble. The poisonous air lapped at his face and he wanted to back away. 'Listen, Morag, I dinna know why . . . But you mustn't say it . . .'

The cat skeleton rattled and its eyes flared brighter. A snap-click and it doubled in size. Howling with laughter, Morag threw her hands at the sky and the darkness rippled with green light. Another harsh clatter and the skeleton doubled again. Black shadow oozed between the bones, making the shape of a wild cat. Its red eyes blinked.

Morag pointed at Niall. 'Kill him,' she said. Then, in Gaelic. 'Kill him! Break his bones!'

'Run, Josh!' Niall spun around. 'Get the others out!'

'I can't leave you!' Josh's face puckered. 'Niall, I can't!'

'You have to! I canna run.' Niall pushed him away. 'Josh, get them out of here!'

Over Niall's shoulder, red eyes flared wide and a hissing, spitting roar ripped from the cat's throat. Its foul breath spread like smoke and Josh spluttered, clamping

122

both hands over his face. He tried to yell, to argue, but the air shattered and tossed him backwards. For a moment, the whole world was bright white. Lightning slammed into the gorge and gorse ignited in green flames. Josh landed on the bridge, Triona under him, Calum on top. Silhouetted against the fire, Mairi clawed back towards the bank.

'Go, Josh!' Niall yelled. 'I'll lead it away.'

Lightning cracked again and Niall stumbled away – white face, white shirt, the cat crouched to spring after him. Morag's shriek was drowned in the cat's roar and the roar was drowned in a single, ear-crippling explosion. The sky came apart and icy rain poured earthwards, grey spears stabbing the darkness. Sobbing, Josh caught Mairi's ankle and wrenched her towards the west bank.

'Mairi!' He fought her clawing hands. 'You've got to come!'

Her mouth gaped wide and Josh knew she must be shrieking, but the gale tore her screams away. The thunder and the hammering rain deafened him. It took all his strength to drag her forwards. Triona and Calum waited, shivering, in the trees. When they saw Mairi's struggles, they hurried to help. Josh forced them into a human chain – himself, Mairi, Triona, Calum. He led the way because he was the strongest, Triona held the chain together, Mairi drifted like a ghost and hardly knew where she was, Calum just did his best to keep up.

The only light was the flash of electricity. Surrounded by wicked, clutching shadows, pounded by rain, Josh aimed his poor gang towards Liath Bealach. If the ground had swallowed him, he could not have cared less. He had lost Niall.

Fearchas waited, white hair whipping his face, the door a

beacon behind him. 'Where's the other bairn?'

Josh's lips were numbed shut. He had to rub them with his fist. 'I messed everything up! You said I'd got to look after Niall . . . I've lost him, again!'

'Easy, laddie . . . Dinna blame yourself . . .'

'Niall couldn't run. Morag set the cat on him. He made it follow him.' Josh gulped, tears burning his cold face. 'He's out there!'

Fearchas heaved the door shut and the room was quiet, warm, full of blue smoke. Calum and Triona collapsed next to the fire.

'Set yourselves down, all of you.' Fearchas lifted his granddaughter's face and spoke to her in Gaelic. She fell against him, bawling. 'There's tea over the fire. Bread and crowdie cheese on the table.'

'I shouldn't have left him!' Josh wailed. 'I shouldn't!'

Fearchas sighed. 'You did right, lad. And he's brave, your friend. You got these three here, out of the storm, on your own, in the dark. That's what you had to do. Niall knew that. If you'd stayed with him, it would be all of you out there. And Niall has to fight for himself now.'

Josh blinked up at the old, Red Indian face. 'Can you stop Morag? Can you make her stop?'

'Her hatred's too strong.' He eased Josh towards the fire, made him sit. 'There's a prophecy about this place – that one of its folk will raise evil to destroy it. And a Dark Outsider will lead the Lone Children to save it. The silver beak was St Domhnall's crow and another's, long before that. It knew the prophecy was coming true, when it picked Niall.'

In a daze, Josh and the others struggled out of their drenched clothes. Fearchas gave them his own things to wear and they huddled together in huge shirts, fishermen's thick socks on their feet. They drank sweet tea out of tin mugs, ate bread and cheese and hardly tasted it.

'Mairi said a boy jumped . . .' Josh frowned, remembering. 'A Triathan boy.'

'Aye, that was before the Vikings, when the Triathans were island chiefs. The chief's son was the silver beak's friend. When another clan tried to kill his father, the lad fled up Feannag Ness. The crow told him to jump over the edge. So, he did.' Fearchas leaned back against the wall, chewing his pipe. 'The birds caught him on their wings and carried him over the island. When the other clan saw it, they made his father their own chief.'

'What about St Domhnall?' Josh asked. 'And the doll?'

'Every year after the laddie flew, island folk threw a doll over Feannag Ness. It was a pagan ceremony, thanking the birds. After the birds saved St Domhnall, the islanders threw St Domhnall dolls, instead. It's all the one story, Josh. The birds saved the saint like they saved the first Triathan lad.'

Josh's face crumpled. 'They haven't saved Niall.'

The cat's breath was pure poison. Niall knew that before he had taken two backward steps. A crack of energy flung him onto the path and his numbed hands buckled. When he wobbled to his feet, the cat's black weight slammed him flat again. Foul breath burned his neck. Claws slashed his sleeve. He remembered, then. Cats played with their prey before they killed.

Where was it? Behind him? In front of him? Hard whips of rain blinded him. He could see no path at all, just blackness, then whiteness. Head down, Niall stumbled faster with no idea where he was going. Grass tangled his feet and he fell into deep mud. This time, the car roared up close and swatted his face. It burned like fire.

Where in the world was he? In the burn? The mud

sucked at his shoes and he wallowed, helplessly. White flash! The cat came at him, howling, and he threw himself away. 'Ach, no!'

The lashing paw caught his ribs, lifted him like a toy and spun him through darkness. Arms and legs clutching at air, he somersaulted and smacked into icy water.

The cold overpowered everything. Gasping, swallowing water, Niall went under.

The cat prowled the water's edge, blacker than the darkness around it, red eyes slit with cruel hunger. It watched the pale boy drowning and roared its fury.

'Come and play!' The cat's thoughts stabbed into Niall's head. 'Come closer! I'll warm you, pale one. Come and play!'

'Ach, my God! I'm in Loch Darach!'

Niall thrashed, wildly, struggling for the shore. No use. Red eyes waited and he fell back, trying to float, his heart hammering his ribs. Rain lashed him, mercilessly. The wind whipped the loch's surface into angry hands, slapping his face. He swallowed water, choking.

If he swam against the current, he would drown, and the cat waited on the shore. Niall closed his eyes. He did not care any more. Too tired. Above the thunder of rain on water, he heard the cat following him. Morag had won.

Something twisted in Niall's chest. Anger. A wave of pure anger filled him and his swollen fingers clenched.

'No! No way, auld witch! I won't die!'

Niall rolled over and forced his arms outwards, juddering through the water. He swam with the current. If he had to swim the whole loch, surely the current must lead to Darachburn? If he could only see a wee glimmer of where he was going . . . His eyes blurred half-shut and his poor, icy toes numbed to nothing. He could be swimming in circles. But he had to swim. Or die.

The four friends lay in Fearchas's big wooden bed, listening to the storm. Mairi and Triona cried themselves to sleep. Josh could not cry any more.

Calum touched his arm. 'Do you think Niall's dead, Josh?'

Josh gasped. 'Don't say that!'

'He's out there on his own with that thing . . . He might die of fright.'

'Calum, shut up!'

'If you'd been hurt, Niall would have stayed with you, Josh, he's that soft-hearted.' Calum sniffed and swallowed. 'So he's right. You're the best Boss. You had to leave him to save Triona and Mairi . . . And me.'

Josh rolled his head on the pillow. Calum's thin face had swollen with crying, the brown eyes reddened and sore. 'Oh yeah? If I'm so good, Calum, how come I feel like a pig? How come I feel so rotten!'

'Maybe you're a touch soft-hearted yourself, Josh.' Calum sniffed, helplessly. 'Like the rest of us.'

Hours must have dragged by. Hours and hours. Niall lay in the cold water and waited to sink for the last time. His chest burned but he was not afraid. He closed his eyes . . .

'Ouch!'

Niall opened his eyes very fast, flailing his arms. He was kneeling on sharp rock. Dizzy, he lifted his head and saw trees. Trees?

'Daft . . .' He spat water. 'Daft-mad and crazy . . .'

But he crawled forwards, eyes glued to those trees. Rocks cut his hands and he hardly felt them. It was a dream. He had died and not noticed. One hand at a time, one knee at a time, he crawled into shallow, lapping waves

and onto a scrubby beach. Sand coated his arms. Trees
. . . Get into the trees . . . Niall swayed onto his feet and
stumbled, head first, over the tangle of tree roots. The
ground hit him, then nothing.

Silence. Niall nodded. He had died. So why did his head
hurt? Everything hurt. Ach, this was unfair! His fingers
and toes throbbed viciously.

'Kerr–ach–ach!'

Something sharp prodded the top of Niall's head and he
tried to swim away then remembered he was in the trees.
A cold, grey-green moon threw a sickly neon light. The
storm was over. Niall blinked forwards and found himself
nose to beak with a small, black-hatted bird. It blinked
back at him and took another peck at his hair.

'Kerr–ach–ach!' It sat on a nest of stones.

'I dinna believe it!' Niall stared between the trees,
counted at least ten other nests. 'You canny wee birdies!
No wonder no one could find you!'

He had found Radcliffe's Tern. He was on Eilean
Sithiche, in the middle of the loch.

'You canny wee birdies . . .'

They were sea birds and would fly for fish every day,
then fly back here to feed their chicks.

The tern tapped Niall's knuckles. 'Kerr–ach–ach.'

'Oh aye! And the same to you!' He sagged back,
grinning. 'You're safe enough here. Yon cat canna swim.'
His eyes closed and he fell into velvet-deep sleep.

Fearchas drove the pony cart through a dreadful, green
silence. During the night, his bird patients had flown. And
poor Mairi could feel nothing against the weight of poison
in the air. She did not know if Niall was dead or alive.

'Look,' Fearchas said. 'The tolleun.'

The tolleun at the road junction had always been the Firinn's responsibility. Mairi had the job of filling the water pots and scattering bread on the stones. Now it lay in pebble-sized fragments. A venomous, green vapour coiled in the wreckage.

'Morag's done it, then.' Fearchas cracked his knuckles, angrily. 'She's really done it!'

The Worm tolleun were just as bad, shattered to rock crumbs. All through Roncamas, over Darachburn and up the lower slope of Feannag Ness, Josh searched for a tall, pale-haired boy. He saw nothing. When he glanced over the harbour, he found bare rocks. The seals had gone as well. Nasty, yellow foam bubbled on the Worm's pebble beach.

So, Morag had won. She hated the island so much, she wanted it turned to poison by the Detritex men. She had used her money to persuade King and MacNeil to help her, then used the poison cat to drive the birds away. So long as birds were on the island, she could not sell. Well, now the birds had gone. She could sell to Detritex and kill the island.

Fearchas parked the trap and everyone clambered out. Josh remembered that Fearchas had not been there for years. For a moment, the old man hesitated, straightening his feathered bowler. Then he followed the four children up the cliff path. As Josh gasped onto the summit, he found the whole island waiting. People had come from every scattered croft to see the birds bring them a new year of luck.

This close, the circle of standing stones looked heavier, impossibly tall and solid. On the far side was the hole in the cliff, a dark passage into the hermit's cell where St Domhnall had lived. Local children had draped the opening with flowers but the blooms had already died, shrivelling into sticky brown decay. Father Kevin sat on a wooden stage to the left of the dead flowers, waiting to say the old words.

Squeezing through the crowd, Josh searched for his dad and Ishbel. But he found the Triathans first. With Fiona's hair bright red, Hector's so pale, they were difficult to miss. When they saw him, they both jumped forwards, hope in their eyes. He could only stare at his feet, ashamed. Fiona broke down, sobbing on Hector's shoulder.

'Josh! Where have you been?' Janet Doinnean grabbed him. 'Are you all safe? Triona . . .?'

'She's bringing Mairi.' Josh shivered. 'We found Niall and lost him again. Where's my dad?'

'With the Balachans.' Janet sighed. 'Every tolleun on the island is poisoned. Here I am, a bird warden, and not a bird in the sky.'

Ishbel came running, Ailsa and Nathan and Willy-John tearing after her. All hugs and kisses, explanations, Calum crying in his mum's arms. The first thing Nathan said was, 'You've found your hat, Josh,' and Josh's eyes filled with tears. Ishbel and Nathan held him between them, hugging him until he could breathe again.

At five to noon, Morag walked onto the flat top of Feannag Ness. Behind her strode Russell King, Harry MacNeil and a man Josh guessed was their boss. Morag scanned the crowd until she found Josh and the others. When she saw that Niall was not there, she smiled.

Fiona screamed. 'Where's my bairn? What have you done with him. Where is he!'

Morag's smile widened and she kept walking until she had reached the VIP's small, wooden stage. To Josh's horror, she climbed the stairs and sat next to Father Kevin. Of course, she owned the island. She was bound to have a seat of honour.

Noon. Father Kevin stepped to the front of the stage. Very quietly, he prayed that the birds would come and give the island luck. For once, he did not get excited or knock things over. He looked terribly upset by it all.

'There's usually a band and singing,' Ishbel said. 'But the bandmaster broke his leg last night, and no one felt much like singing when they breathed this air.'

'I'd love to take that crooked smirk off Morag's face!' Nathan gave Josh a sudden, hard hug. 'We were up at dawn looking for you, worried sick. Fearchas, thanks for looking after Josh.'

Fearchas nodded. 'It was time for me to come back, if only to see it all die. You've a fine brave lad, there. He brought my Mairi home. I'll no forget that.'

A boy stepped from behind the stage – a kid from Class Four – and walked shakily through the stone circle to the cliff edge. Nothing in front of him but green sky and the long drop onto the rocks. Josh felt sorry for him. No one had wanted to take Niall's place. The boy yelled the Gaelic words at the sick light swamping the bay.

'Poor bairn . . .' Ishbel translated, quickly: 'Each June, we thank you for the luck of the last year. Now we call you to bless the year to come. We give you this son of Earth to show that we remember. Birds, rise to the air and bring us your wings of life.'

The boy flung the cloth doll as far as he could, out over the water. Absolutely nothing happened.

'Your bird friends have gone.' Morag stood to face the crowd. 'There's not a seal in the harbour, not an otter in the burns. There'll be inspectors and the like to prove me right, then I'll sell this place.' Her twisted mouth quivered. 'You'll no forget the Falamhs, any of you!'

11 The Birds

'Kerr-ach-ach!'

A bird pecked Niall awake and he mumbled at it to shut up. When it pecked him, again, he groaned and rolled over.

'What's wrong with you? Ouch!' Niall clutched his throat. Screaming for hours, then being drowned, had done it no good at all. He sounded like a strangled frog. Pairs of birds watched him. 'You should be off catching your breakfast . . .'

Staggering upright was a mistake. He yelped, choked, and fell down again. His poor ankles felt broken, his jeans were ripped through, his shirt shredded. The left side of his face had stiffened and his fingers trembled, tracing the four cruel scars. Scarred for life. It hurt and he swallowed tears.

Across the loch, green mist swirled in snake-long waves, covering all the land. The birds had not wanted to cross it and he could not blame them.

'The time!' Niall's watch slopped half-full of muddy water. But he knew, anyway. It was too late.

'Ach, no. How could this happen?' He sagged back against a tangle of tree roots and a tern hopped onto his grazed knee. 'There, then . . . Are you no afraid of me?' He stroked its wing and it kerr-ached at him.

That odd feeling came back. He had warned Morag not

132

to set her cat on him. What a daft, idiotic thing to say! She would have expected him to beg for his life. But he felt it now. It had meant something.

'I'll tell you something, bird. You're lucky we protect you. I could eat twenty of yon eggs, I'm that starved.'

With a last stroke of the bird's neck, Niall scrabbled to his feet. Loch Darach glinted all around him, holding the green mists back. But for how long? In stockinged feet, bare toes poking through the wool, Niall tottered into the water. A last glance at the Redcliffe's Terns' sharp red beaks and he slid forwards into the loch.

The previous night had taught Niall one thing, there was no point in fighting Darach's icy current. He had always been the long distance type, not the sprinter. If he fought for the shore, he would drown. But he could swim for a very long time if the dark waters carried him.

Two hours later, Niall crawled out of Loch Darach and flopped onto his back. His first breath sucked poison into his battered throat and he squirmed sideways, choking. Immediately to his right lay the wreckage of a tolleun and the crushed stone oozed slow, green slime.

'Ach, that's truly horrendous! Look at that muck!' He coughed harder. 'Morag . . . You stupid auld witch!'

The path to Roncamas followed Darachburn due south. Every sharp stone found its way into Niall's socks and he tugged the unravelling wool off. Within five minutes, he had cut his big toe to the bone. Within twenty, he was sobbing with every limping step. When he put his weight on his feet, the pain stabbed through his arches and into his ankle-joints. He left red smears in the mud. But he could not stop. He had to reach Feannag Ness before dusk. Dusk divided day from night and Morag had used dusk to raise her poison cat. One way or another, it would all end before nightfall.

Mairi stiffened. Around her, people hung their heads and talked in whispers. Islanders crowded every room in the Worm, but no one was smiling. Mairi slithered her way to the window. Outside, the green light darkened. Morag was at the helipad, behind the hospital, saying her good-byes to the Detritex boss.

Mairi stared across Roncamas bay, up to the silhouette of Na Bodaich – a rough, black crown of rocks against the green sky. She screamed.

'Mairi?' Josh got to her first. 'What?'

She just pointed. A boy stood on the cliff edge, pale hair, pale face, tall and still as a ghost. Josh grabbed her hand and ran for the door.

'As soon as we prove there's no wildlife on the island, I'll invite you over to sign the contract.' The Detritex boss did not offer Morag his hand to shake. He twitched a look at the sky and dived into the safety of the helicopter. 'Our workforce will be living here, while we store the waste. I hope this place isn't unhealthy.'

Morag raised her brows at him. 'It will be less healthy when you've dumped your poisons.' The helicopter door slammed and she turned to King and MacNeil. 'Well, now? Is this all quick enough for you? I worked hard enough, last night.'

King frowned. 'I don't want to know about last night. That was our agreement. I don't want to hear anything about it. Ever.'

'This place stinks.' MacNeil coughed. 'It's going straight to my bronchitis.'

Morag smirked at him. 'You'd no feel it so much if you

weren't a smoker. And nothing will live here soon. Poison's leaking from the rock into the sea. There'll be dead fish on the beaches tomorrow.' She stretched her arms, watching the helicopter whirr out of sight. 'And I want us back at the house before dusk.'

'What's the hurry?' MacNeil asked. 'There's no one here to rush you.'

'Maybe not.' She shook her head. 'I'm no taking chances.'

'Who's that?' King pointed to the small figure on Feannag Ness. 'They don't leave the poor kid up there all night, do they?'

'The doll laddie was dark.' MacNeil glanced at Morag. 'That one's pale. And I'd no forget that hair, after I lugged him down the well.'

King nodded. 'Well, thank God for that. I thought you'd killed him, the way you knocked him about . . .' He stared after Morag. 'Hey, where are you going?'

Niall sat on the stone roof of St Domhnall's cell, hugging his poor feet and watching the lighthouse flash fade from white to yellow-green. He was cold to the bone and his scarred face throbbed. The sun slid lower in the sky, staining the rocks and the zigzag steps cut into the cliff wall. Those rescue steps helped folk caught by the tide. In another hour, they would vanish into darkness. One hour. He was going to do something terrible. He hoped he did not upset too many people.

Mairi had seen him first. Niall had watched the cart leave the Worm as if wolves were after it. He knew his mam and dad would have begged to come, but Fearchas was a canny auld man. He had persauded them to wait. Morag had seen Niall shortly after. Even as he watched, the Detritex car raced through Roncamas. It would arrive a few minutes after Fearchas.

Josh led the way up the cliff path, for the second time in one day, heading higher into the green glow above Feannag Ness. His lungs burned in his chest. Then he heard a car skid to a halt behind him.

'Morag! I know it is!'

Gasping, he thundered onto the cliff-top.

Fearchas caught Josh's arm. 'Don't try to go to Niall, Josh. He has to be on his own for this.'

'OK.' Josh hesitated. 'You know what's going to happen?'

'I might.' Fearchas pushed him forward. 'Go on, now. They're right behind us.'

If Morag was following him, Josh wanted some nice heavy stones between her and the gang. He dragged Mairi to the east side of the circle, where he could peer through the stones one way to Niall, the other way to Morag. Fearchas stopped a couple of strides away, chewing his empty pipe.

Mairi stared at Niall's pale back. 'Josh . . . I shout?'

'No . . . Wait.'

Calum shuddered. 'Man, he looks that cold! Look at his shirt! And his poor wee feet! There's blood dripping from his toes!'

'Triathan!' Morag stumbled to the edge of the circle. 'You've lost! Where are your bird friends.'

Niall slid off the Saint's cell and turned. Josh gasped. Only the poison cat could have clawed those ragged scars in his face. Then Josh remembered them. He had seen them in the Worm pool. And, when Niall spoke, it was not with his old voice. Softer, huskier, but suddenly unafraid, the new voice floated through the stones to Morag Falamh.

'The birds are waiting for me, Morag.'

'Ach, don't talk daft!' She sneered at him. 'There are no birds here.'

'Well, apart from Radcliffe's Tern.' Niall met her eyes. 'There's a whole flock of them on Eilean Sithiche. That's where I slept, last night.'

'You're a liar!' Spit ran down her chin. 'Liar!'

'Not that it matters, mind,' Niall said. 'This poison is what matters.'

Morag laughed. 'And there's no court on earth would believe it's to do with me.'

Triona glared at her. 'But there's the post office fire! And there's Cashel kidnapping Niall . . .'

'Your word against ours.' MacNeil smiled at Josh. 'How's the ears?'

'We've got proof!' Josh felt Calum's hand on his arm and he was glad. MacNeil still frightened him. 'You'll all go inside . . . Prison . . . Forever.'

'Ach, you watch too much television, lad!' MacNeil snapped. 'There's no proof at all.'

'There is, too.' Calum nodded towards Niall. 'Niall was locked in Cashel's car boot. And the car's still near the harbour. I bet the boot's full of Niall's hair. And there'll be Niall's blood all over the place, down that well of yours. If the lid's still padlocked and Niall's too big to fit through the hole I went down, you *had* to have put him in. We don't have television on the island, but I've read books. I know about police scientists . . .' Calum rattled on, breathlessly. 'Just because we're on an island doesn't mean we're all dafties. And when they catch Cashel, he'll tell them everything.'

Josh grinned. 'Nice one, Calum.'

King turned on Morag, furious. 'I told you we shouldn't have done that! Nothing they could prove, I said! You should have known Cashel would run for it!'

Fearchas stepped forwards. Morag had not seen him until then and she recoiled, cursing.

'Well, Morag Falamh.' He nodded to her. 'Do you think yon man in his helicopter will sign anything when he knows you kidnap children?'

'Maybe not.' She rested her head against the stone, her twisted mouth bitter. 'But if I died right now, I'd take the island with me. Forget your Radcliffe's Terns, Triathan. They'll starve or die of poisoned fish within a week.'

Niall limped forwards. His voice rang icy cold. 'It's dusk, Morag.'

'Aye?' She flinched, then controlled herself. 'What if it is?'

'Did your cat no come home, last night? Where's your big bonny cat? There's no circle around you now.'

Morag's face paled, her wet chin glinting green. She suddenly looked afraid. 'You dinna know anything! You've no powers!'

'But the crow gave me something to remember. If you call that cat out of its bones and tell it to kill, it canna rest until it has. It's tasted my blood, it won't fancy that again. Now it's coming for yours and there's no circle to protect you.'

'Josh!' Triona nudged him. 'Look . . . there's folk all around the harbour.'

Tiny faces lined the sea-wall, turned up towards Feannag Ness. The whole island, Josh thought, waiting in the dim green between day and night. He felt as if he stood at the edge of the world. Ten minutes and it would all end, turn poison green and crumble under his feet.

Mairi gasped and shrank into Josh's side. Down on the

marshes, something splashed towards them. The first time Josh had seen the cat, it had hardly been real, just shadow and claw. The second time, it had been huge and heavy with life. Now it was monstrous, three metres tall, with claws like curled knives. Its fur sparked and glistened. Pure evil. As Josh watched, the dark shape bounded over the heather, mashing it flat, huge strides carrying it past Roncamas school, on to the lower slopes of Feannag Ness.

'Josh.' Niall gazed at him, ghostly pale. 'Once the cat has killed, it's finished, but we'd no lose the poison. I've got to decide for myself, this time.'

'Niall, don't you do anything stupid!' Josh's skin wriggled into gooseflesh. 'You listen to me, Niall!' Mairi's nails dug into his hand and he swivelled back to the hill. Red eyes glittered closer. A stink of death swept over the wet grass. And Morag gave a horrible, petrified shriek.

'Ach, no! No!' Gaelic tumbled from her mouth.

'What's she saying?' Josh tugged Mairi's arm. 'What's she saying?'

'Rubbish.' Mairi shook her head. 'It's rubbish.'

The giant cat leapt onto the cliff top, tail lashing the air. Hungry eyes blazed over the horrified faces watching it, searching . . .

'Dinna move!' Fearchas hissed. 'Stand steady!'

The cat found its prey and snarled red hatred at the woman who had called it from its bones.

Morag had the old stones at her back and, as the cat's lips curled from its teeth, she slithered into the grass. Slobbering and snorting, horrible, senseless noises in her mouth, Morag Falamh curled into a ball of bone and thin skin. One bite for her poison cat. Its jaws opened, teeth glinting green. The vile stink of it drove Josh back.

Niall clapped his hands, an echoing crack. 'Come on, I'm here. Come on, poison cat. Come and play.'

Josh tried to run forwards but Fearchas caught him around the waist. For one aching second, he saw Niall's face very clearly, saw the weird, half-smile on it. Then the cat roared through the circle of stones, leaping for Niall's throat.

Niall yelled: 'Na h-eoin!'

He arched backwards and jumped, like a high-board diver, head first over the cliff edge.

A burst of air crushed Josh back into Fearchas's arms. Screaming, a train-whistle, a screeching-brakes of a sound exploded upwards. Clapping. No, flapping! A million wings soared from the caves below Feannag Ness. Every bird on the island – gulls and crows, golden eagles and terns, grey-lag geese from Loch Sioda, shelduck and hen harriers and black guillemots – every bird there was or had been or would be – ghosts of dead birds like blue flames and shadows of birds not even in their eggs, thin as tissue paper – poured up with the gale. Birds white as sea-water spray, warm feathers, bright eyes and claws, open, squealing beaks and hot blood. Living birds tore into the green light.

Fierce blue fire licked the edges of St Domhnall's old cell, flushing the poison away. Tearing upwards, the wind unravelled Mairi's plaits, dragged at her skirts. It plucked Fearchas's bowler hat like an apple. Blades of grass whipped past, whole clumps spun upwards. Triona's woolly bunches stood on end and Calum almost blew away.

Josh jumped at a blue crack of energy from one of the coastguards' tolleun. He swivelled in time to see the other spit blue flame. Across the bay, the two Worm tolleun ignited, blue fire burning upwards, everything upwards. Josh tottered back, staring at the pillar of green light covering the island, spinning with birds, higher and higher, all of the poison sucked into space.

The wind died and Josh fell flat onto Fearchas's boot.

'Whoohhhh!' Gasping for breath, Calum in his lap, Josh remembered. 'Niall! Get up, Calum! Move!'

King and MacNeil took off in the opposite direction, sprinting, terrified, down the hill to their car. From head to foot, they were both plastered in rotting mud, grass and black slime.

'Come on, Calum!'

No green. The lighthouse glow swung over the harbour brilliant white, and the gleaming, silver moon glow shone down onto the rocks. Niall lay there, still as death.

'Down the steps!' Triona ran. 'Down the rescue steps! Come on!'

They stumbled down the rocky stairs, only speed keeping them upright. Josh wanted to be first and barged past Tree on one of the corners, but Mairi jumped from half-way up the last flight, her loosened plaits swiping his face. She ran like a racehorse until a metre away from Niall's body, then skidded to a halt.

Josh stared down at his friend. Broken white feathers knotted his hair, grey feather-fluff clung to his tattered jeans. A slow trickle of blood ran from his mouth. His face was white, the cat scratches raw red and swollen.

Calum sat down. 'He's dead.'

Niall sat up. 'Ach, I feel truly horrendous . . .'

Josh screamed. 'You! You should be dead! You . . . You . . .'

'I feel truly awful.' Niall slithered sideways, gripping the seat of his jeans. 'My backside's scraped raw . . . What am I sitting on?'

Josh knelt beside him, breathing hard. 'Well, you're lying on rocks, for a start! They should have broken you

141

into little pieces! And lumps of . . .' He tore his hand back.

Mairi touched the jagged, white lumps. 'Cat bone.' She looked at Niall's poor face. 'Cat . . . all bone broken. Your face scratch. Cat scratch.' Her eyes filled with tears and she twisted away from him.

'I'm sorry, Mairi. I had to call the birds.' Niall looked guilty. 'I knew Josh would no let me, if I asked him.'

'Too right! I thought you were dead!' Josh glared at Triona. 'Stop giggling!'

'I canna . . . stop.' Triona sat down, head on her bony knees, and howled with laughter.

Mairi slid as close to Niall as she could and started to re-plait her hair. 'Your . . . talk . . .'

'Voice,' Josh said.

Mairi nodded. 'Niall, voice good . . . I like it.'

For the first time in two days, Niall's face lost its white glow. He blushed.

Calum stirred the bones with one finger. 'Man, this is gruesome! Someone should pick this up and burn it. Gruesome!'

From a great height, the crow with the silver beak let itself fall clumsily onto Niall's shoulder. It nearly fell right off again, flapping off balance. It prodded his neck then shrugged, losing dust and feathers.

'Now, I'm no so sure I'm speaking to you, Crow.' Niall touched the ragged wings. 'He let it happen. You know that, Josh? He was around all the time but he let it happen.'

Josh looked at the big bird. It had saved him on the ferry. It had showed him the other entrance to the well. But Niall was right, it could have flown down the day Cashel snatched him from the school. It could have warned them.

142

'Maybe it had to happen,' Josh said. 'Maybe you had to jump to stop Morag once and for all.'

'Morag!' Niall's eyes widened. 'Ach, my God! I'd forgotten all about her . . .'

Niall turned towards the rescue steps and Josh followed his eyes. Slowly, shakily, Fearchas walked towards them. His white hair stood on end.

'That poor, foolish woman is quite mad. Seeing the cat come up the hill for her . . . It probably turned her mind.'

'I think . . . I think I knew it would.' Niall put a hand towards Josh but Mairi grabbed it first. He struggled to his feet, leaning on her shoulder. 'I'm bruised black and blue. Every inch of me. And my feet . . .!' Tears glittered in his eyes and he swallowed hard. 'Is it bad of me, Fearchas? I knew Morag would no stand seeing the cat up close. It was a frightening thing.'

'She deserved it.' Triona stopped laughing. 'Dinna you feel sorry for her, Niall! She deserves to go crazy!'

'Nay, lass, we're no judge and jury.' Fearchas glanced up at the stone circle. 'You used her own weapon against her, Niall. That feels mighty right, to me. If she dies, there's no guilt on our heads. And then, heaven help this poor island!'

'What?' Josh hauled himself up. 'What, if Morag dies? I thought no one knew what would happen?'

'I got to see auld MacRath's will. When my lad died, I had legal papers to sign. I went to the mainland and the poor fool in the law office told me Morag kept her papers there. I told him I'd crack his head unless he gave me a sight of that will.'

Josh stared at him. 'What did it say?'

'When the last Falamh dies, the island passes to the Five Families. That was what MacRath wanted. Morag has no kin. So the island passes . . .' Fearchas let his Red Indian face crease into a smile. 'I suppose it goes to you bairns.'

'Wow!' Josh watched Calum making piles of cat bones, Mairi daring to hold Niall's arm, Triona grinning. He met Niall's eyes. 'Hey! That's really neat!'

Niall smiled. 'Aye, Josh. Really neat. Do you think I can go home, now? My mam and dad must be worn ragged with worry.'

Something hit the back of Josh's head. He spun around, ready to defend himself. Spog squealed at him and fastened her webbed claws to his shirt. He remembered that he was the Boss and stood tall, trying to look cool.

'Yeah, right . . . Your mum and dad will be well pleased.' He grinned again. 'Boss of the island! I mean . . .' He saw Niall's eyes close. 'All five of us will be. The gang will be . . . But I'm the Boss, aren't I?'

Spog chose that moment to stick her tail in his face.

Calum laughed. 'Aye, Boss.'

Triona. 'Aye, Boss.'

Mairi smiled at him. 'Aye, Josh.'

And Niall. 'You'll have to carry me up those steps, you know . . . Boss.'